HOME GROWN STORIES & HOME FRIED LIES

Mitch Jayne
of The Dillards

Words With The Bark On Them
& Other Ozark Oddments

Designed and Illustrated by Diana Jayne

WILDSTONE MEDIA

Jayne, Mitch
Home Grown Stories and Home Fried Lies:
Words With The Bark On Them and Other Ozark Oddments

ISBN - 1-882467-30-2
Library of Congress Catalog Card # 99-76941

Designed and Illustrated by Diana Jayne ©2000

Wildstone Media
PO Box 511580
St. Louis, MO 63151
www.wildstonemedia.com

Contents

Contents

—Long as a well rope, but purposely so—

This book is dedicated to a whole bunch of people. I have changed some names in the stories, knowing that some folks don't like appearing in books, but used real names when the characters were either dead or so good-humored they didn't mind being a part of printed history. When in doubt about either of these things, I picked a name that worked and if one of these turns out to be yours, it's unintentional.

I want to thank Lee Floyd and Dr. Donna Jayne who both took the time to share with me their families and distant kin, and I want to thank Carole and Valerie, my daughters who were never shy (thank God) about sharing their wildly various friends with their dad.

I want to thank my publisher Dan Randant and his wife Mary who welcomed me into their lives and invested a lot of time in our friendship and my writing. Dan is responsible for this book no matter how vigorously he tries to deny it.

I want to thank Dean Webb, Rodney and Douglas Dillard for all the years we have played together as The Dillards and laughed a lot at each other as friends. Whatever else we have done, we have always brought out the best in each other and shared our music with everyone we could get to listen.

I guess most of all I dedicate this book to the people of the Ozarks, my dependable friends who have let me write and talk about them any way I chose over the years, believing that I meant well and couldn't help myself when I saw the funny side of almost everything. These include the storytellers old and young, male and female, who have kept up the tradition of the story itself, passing things on through their children and allowing me to listen in.

Without people like Lester Adamick who insisted on building both my house and belief in myself; Howe Teague, who made me a storyteller; Mary Carnett, who thought I was trustworthy; Jimmy Butler, who let me sit by his stove on winter days; Roger Dillon, who asked me to write a column for his newspaper *The Current Wave*; and Kathy Love, who edited the *Missouri Conservationist* magazine to its lasting benefit and liked my work, I might have turned into either an Otis-class drunkard or a Republican.

Thanks too, to those good friends who I can't name without this dedication getting totally out of hand, but like the people in the stories, know who they are.

I must add, of course, that this book was written with and for my wife Diana who loved the Ozarks and its people at first meeting and couldn't wait to draw the things you see here. To paraphrase Briscoe Darling; "She may have a Texas haircut but her heart was shaped in a bowl."

Finally, I would like to dedicate this book to my small nephew, Mitchell Clark, who will hopefully carry a Missouri sense of family and humor into this new century, which I suspect will need it.

I have written several books, but this is the first one I have written for the fun of it. I just have all this Ozark funny stuff in my head, circling like the buzzard that just ate Wino Fred and can't fly straight.

As far as I know, nobody actually reads one of these introductions until they have skimmed a book enough to see if they want to buy it. It's a whole lot like buying a hound from a stranger; you'd rather look at the hound first to see if he's bird-billed, or narrow chested, or blind, before you need particulars about the seller.

But if you are actually reading this, my suggestion would be to flip some pages and see if there's anything that looks like fun to you. If not, you're driving your ducks to a poor puddle, as we say at home. You should save your investment because you really don't want to know more about me. Knowing too much about me could seriously affect your chances of running for public office sometime.

See, fun is pretty much what I had in mind when I wrote all this down. I've lived 70 years on this planet, looking for excuses to laugh, and by the time you're halfway through this you'll know more about what made me laugh than anybody from someplace besides Missouri would need to.

Remember this is educational material, and after use should be disposed of in a safe and appropriate manner, i.e., give it to somebody from Arkansas.

Mitch Jayne

Webster's American Heritage dictionary definition:

Ozark Mountains (o´zärk).

A range of low mountains (1,500 to 2,500 feet) spreading over an area of 60,000 square miles in southwestern Missouri, northwestern Arkansas, and eastern Oklahoma.

Mitch Jayne's Definition Of The Ozarks

Wonderful old hills, yawning with age and satisfied to lie there comfortably under the sun. Worn down like old hound's teeth, the Ozarks are all done with the battles fought by young mountains like the Rockies and the Sierras. The oldest mountains on the continent, the Ozarks are furred with oak and hickory and time, and are as serene about their clear, frisky rivers as old animals are with the new litter playing across their bellies.

The Ozarks have captured time in a net and intend to turn it loose when they've measured and weighed it, like some considerate fisherman. The springs of the Ozarks are as clear and deep and startlingly blue as morning glories, the rivers run as transparent as gin, and the people who live in such a place can't help reflecting the satisfaction of it. Ozarkers speak in words as colorful as autumn leaves and use terms as carefully preserved as paw paw jelly or persimmon wine. We laugh a lot because we have been allowed a lot of joy.

The Ozarks is a thoughtful place because nobody ever found it by accident. The people who settled there did it out of choice, giving up one thing to accept another, their reward being a land beyond any sort of tick-tock time. It remains a place where old things are allowed to stay because they are welcome and still valuable.

The Ozarks are the mountains where America chose to store its nostalgia for the forgotten pioneers, the smoke of hickory fires, the sound of fiddles and the far off cry of hounds.

But most of all, the Ozarks is our lasting, bittersweet memory of how most Americans used to be.

A Ozark Words

Abundance *Large amount —*
"Hit shore takes an abundance of gooseberries to comprise a gallon."

Affeared *Worried, afraid —*
"I'm much affeared dad won't make it to spring."

Afore *Before —*
"Hit'll rain afore daylight; the whippoorwills has heshed."

Against *In preparation for —*
"You best bank that fire good against morning."

Air *Are —*
"They ain't many of us left, air they?"

Ary *Any —*
"Have you seen ary deer this year?"
"Nary one, boys!"

Ask after *Inquire about —*
"Ma told me be sure and ask after your cousin Bess."

Atwixt *Between —*
"He's lost his reason, atwixt one thing and another."

Aver *Swear (take oath) —*
"She was puny last week but I seen her on the square and she avers she's better now."

Chapter One

Here's How All This Started

In 1951 I went down to the Ozark Mountains of Missouri to teach one room schools. I was raised in the northern part of the state but I wasn't a fanatic about it and wasn't above improving myself. What happened was, I met a girl from the Ozarks who had come up to go school at the University of Missouri in Columbia. She not only used words I had never heard spoken, she told me about going to one room schools in the mountains where her mother taught. This girl was pretty, but where she was from was <u>beautiful</u>. She described a place where the rivers were clear as gin and where there were blue springs you could sink a church in. A place, she said, where everybody and their Aunt Mattie could play an instrument of some kind—except maybe an accordion—and they held play parties and square dances all the time. She said that everybody was neighborly, the old people told stories, everybody hunted all the time and gigged fish at night. She told me that there were a few old time purists who still made moonshine whiskey.

I wanted to marry that girl in the worst way. I wanted to move down among all those people and live like that and maybe make a living writing wonderful stories. I intended to become a writer, so I also wanted to find out what all the words this girl used meant. I wanted to live among people who used them, because words were going to be what I made a living at. I loved words then as much as I do now, 50 years later, and I think it was words I fell in love with enough to actually get married. There are all manner of reasons to marry someone, and humans use up most of them, which of course reminds me of a story.

*I*t was old man Wickard's story about how he married Myrtle. Old man Wickard was a neighbor of mine during one of the few times I lived in town and he had this nice wife Myrtle who looked like everybody's grandma.

"Well, I was runnin' moonshine whiskey, over in Indiany" he told me one night, "and me and this other feller had took a couple of girls along for the company. Had a trunk load of Kentucky whiskey and was taking it to Terry-Haute, you see. Had to keep to the back roads dodging the laws and never went near no towns or nothing. Well, we was having a big old time drinking, you know, filling those girls up with big lies and moonshine and finally we had to stop because all of us had to pee. Well, the other girl she went over to the ditch and squatted, but Myrtle, my girl, she just stood up there with us two men, just like a little rooster, you know.

"I says, 'Myrtle what are you a-doing?' and she jist reached down and grabbed hold of her twitchet some way and kind of cocked her leg up and pissed plumb over three strands of bob wire fence. I'd never seen anything like it in my life. So then we went on to Terry-Haute and got married."

Besides not ever being able to look at Myrtle quite the same way again, I remember thinking that was about the strangest reason for getting married I ever heard of. I don't know if it was any better or worse than mine, but whatever the reason, lots of us got married back then, after World War II and some lasted, some didn't. When I married, had children and finally went down to the Ozarks to teach a one room school myself, I found out from one of my backwoods scholars that wisdom about such things gets passed on, which reminds me of another story. (Which I can see is going to be a problem here. This book's liable to be longer than the Missouri Wildlife Code.)

I once was teasing one of my sixth graders at a school party where a little girl was dressed up in her best. I said, "My, Mildred, are you getting all triggered up to get some boy to marry you?"

She said, in all seriousness, "Oh no, Mr. Jayne.
I ain't going to marry too soon to the wrong feller
and have to set on the blister for 50 years!"

But wait now, I'm getting ahead of myself, which I have a tendency to do. I want to tell you how I got my first school and how I began to learn some of the words I've sprinkled through this book, figuring if I don't fling them in front of you, nobody else will. The words are still there, but if you want to hear most of them nowadays you'll have to buy you a fox or a coon hound and go listen to the old men around a hunting fire, who still say things like; "There's an abundance of turkeys this year," or "I aver, they's so many of them, they're in each other's way. I'm gonna have to stock a bushel of shells against turkey season."

Mae Deatherage, my new mother-in law, who in her day had taught a dozen of these schools told me how you went about teaching eight grades in one room, actually teaching or 'reciting' one class at a time, while giving the others something to study. The way she explained it was that everyone in the room heard whatever was going on, whether they wanted to or not, and even though they were doing their own assignments in work books or reading on their own, knowledge was flowing all around them. The smart ones would pick up on lots more than you were teaching in any one grade. A fourth grader who had a knack for math, for instance, could tune in on what 6th graders were learning and wouldn't get bored with simple stuff. Mae made it sound like a great challenge and I couldn't wait to try it.

Mae also told me about the hardships of teaching during the depression years, the lack of money for books, the politics of getting a school when a school board would rather hire a relative, the extra work of building fires in winter, and killing copperhead snakes in summertime. She told about having to get to school by boat when the rivers were up, teaching big country boys twice her size and "mean with it," as she said. Then there were disagreements with school board members and parents who thought she was partial to one child over another, and a dozen or so other problems that would come up. She talked about rough Ozark families from back in the hills who "fit, shot and throwed hatchets, and blackguarded at the dinner-table." The kind of people, she warned me, who could make a school teacher's life miserable. I didn't care as long as people didn't set fire to the school house or play the accordion, I thought I could cope with any outrageous behavior.

Mae said that as far as she knew Shannon County only abounded in banjo pickers and fiddlers. My father-in-law added that "there were so many fiddlers down there, their feet were sticking out the winders." I did love to hear my in-laws talk. The more I heard, the

6

more I wanted to go and live among people who never used just one adjective if they could string together twenty for the same price.

So one broiling hot August day in the middle of my fourth year of college, I loaded up my wife and two small children and set out for the Ozarks to apply for a teaching job in a one room school. I soon found out all the schools in Shannon County had filled all the teaching positions. So I went to Dent County and checked in with the Superintendent of schools.

The Superintendent was a white headed old man named Walter Jenkins who had his office in the ancient courthouse and I remember that when I walked in, all the big windows were open and Walter was in his short sleeves, swatting flies with a rolled up copy of *The Salem Post*.

This set my worries about my lack of education and experience at rest, because Walter might have been higher up the educational pile than I was, but I knew enough that I would have shut the windows before I started killing flies.

Walter had one school left, "open for a schoolmaster," he told me. "Now it's back in the jillikins," he warned, "and it's a very poor deestrict. Not many chirren for scholars." Lord, I didn't care about <u>that</u>. I'd already heard four old fashioned Ozark words in one sentence and made a mental note to jot them down the minute I got back to my car. I knew my kind of country when I heard it.

I found out about "Jilikins" almost immediately since that is where he sent me to find my school. "Back in the Jilikins" means (in the Ozarks), wild country where most of the roads are laid out by deer or a lost woodcutter.

On my way to finding this one room school where I would begin my first teaching job I got turned around, then confused and eventually completely lost. I had never seen such a stand of timber with unmarked gravel tracks heading in every direction. Not one house or a living soul had I seen for over an hour until finally, just before I figured the road was going to peter out into a gopher hole, I found a little clearing. There was a house and, praise God, a woman picking a chicken in the front yard. I don't remember which of us was the gladdest to see the other.

I said, "Pardon me, Ma'am, could you tell me where Cross School on Horse Creek would be? She had one of those voices that could worm a sheep and once started she rattled on like she'd been wound up the night before.

"Well now, lemme see, Cross School, seems like I should-a heerd my old man tell about it, he goes most ever-whur coon huntin' and all, but I don't have no knowance of it myself, I don't b'leeve, bein's as I stay here at the house most of the time. Now I hate to say no to a

stranger, don't seem right, but I cain't memorize him a-talking about it ary time. Now he's
out after a cow and if he was here you could
quiz him about it but there's no telling when he'll be home the way
that breachy thang won't stay inside of a fence, I declare! Now not
to give ye no short ainswer, but I
hain't no idee. But you keep on this
way till the road tears and if you
cleave to the left you'll come to
another house and you ask that
lady, Miz Parker? She's liable
to know on account of her
man works at the M F and
A store in Rolly and if ary
person knows, now he'd
know."

Well, I thanked
her and drove off,
grateful that she'd
run out of wind,
but I hadn't gone a
hundred yards un-
til I saw her in my
rear view mirror,
waving frantically.
Standing next to
her was a tall man,

9

waving his cowboy hat. I backed all the way to them, through all that dust that I had just freshly made, and rolled down the window. Her husband just had two upper fangs for teeth, far enough apart to punch notebook paper, and grinned at me with them.

"This here's my old man," said the lady proudly, "and he don't know either."

I don't know how I got off on all that, since I was aiming to tell you about my first school, but this is my book and I can tell it any way I want. Besides, if I can still remember every word that old woman said, you could at least have the patience to learn the language.

There's plenty more to follow...

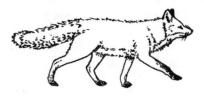

B Ozark Words

Bait *A sufficient amount —*
"*Some eats boughten vittles, but I always take a bait of dinner in a poke.*"

Beastes *Plural of Beasts —*
"*My Pa ain't much at plantin' crops but he's awful good with the beastes.*"

Beguile *To pass the time pleasantly -also- to charm —*
"*He smokes that old pipe to beguile the time.*"

Beleaguer *Belabor —*
"*Don't never argue religion with him, he'll beleaguer ever point under the sun and jower about it all day.*"

Bemean *To criticize -or- demean —*
"*To bemean another man's dog thataway ain't fit'n manners.*"

Benasty *To befoul one's britches —*
"*That kid's too young to go to school. He's liable to benasty his britches.*"

Blackguard *Profane -or- vulgar talk —*
"*Mama won't have us blackguard in the house.*"

Breachy *Cannot keep fenced in —*
"*That old breachy cow keeps me fixin' fence all the time.*"

Chapter Two
Cross School

Cross School, once I found it, wasn't much to look at, but by that time neither was I. I won't go into all the hunting up of board members it took to sign me up as schoolmaster; the drives through dusty hay fields where grasshoppers as big as cigars bounced off the

 windshield, the stops at farmhouses where tiny children lined up to stare at me like owls, and suspicious yard dogs that wet down my tires. There were hill farms so steep you could fall out of a cornfield and break a leg. There were hollows so dark, a board member who lived in one told me, "The rooster has to fly up a hunderd feet to know when to crow fer day."

It's enough to say that all these folks were glad to see me because they'd about given up on getting a teacher for Cross School. Finally, I went to see the president of the board who lived in an old log house and could neither read nor write. He signed his name to my 'warrant' with a flourish, copying it off an old check someone had written him, and shook my hand like pumping well water. I was hired for $250 a month to be the schoolmaster of Cross School, with its 15 scholars, a bookcase full of texts that were printed in Hoover's time, a Charter Oak stove with rusty pipe that wobbled 40 feet to an old hazard of a chimney. Then there was the well that had gone dry two years back and four big mantle lamps for lighting. Included in the assets of the school were two ancient privies, whitewashed I figured to make them stand up. One was marked girls, one was marked boys, and that was as far as plumbing concerned itself at Cross School. Shucks, I didn't care. I was now a school teacher and about anything I did would have to be an improvement, I thought.

By the first day of school I had done all my homework. I had gone to a teacher's conference in Rolla and had picked out all the new texts and workbooks the decrepit treasury of District No. 8 of Dent County could afford. Supply shopping for Cross School was a whole lot like trying to feed a big family on a pound of hamburger; it could be done but it took invention.

I got to meet other one room school teachers at that convention and was jarred to find out there were only two other men there. School boards didn't favor male teachers much. Doan Black, my board president confided to me, "on account of some of 'em's bad to use the hick'ry on scholars." His questioning tone was gently polite, but I could tell he wanted to know how I felt about whipping kids. I said I didn't believe in it.

"I've always heard," he said mildly, "that you can't teach nobody nothing by hitting them on the rear end. That's not the end you're after." I made a note of that.

I was to learn more from the women teachers I met than the other men, who both seemed to me a little straitlaced and "full of themselves," as Ozarkers put it. The women were mostly housewives who'd had a year or two of college and were pretty laid back about this business of teaching children. One of these middle age teachers told me:

"Teaching a one room school is a lot like slinging mud at a wall, only you're flingin' information. What misses one mark will still hit another. You'll find out nothing's wasted."

It didn't sound very romantic, but it made sense.

On my first morning at the little school on Horse Creek I decided to make friends if I could. I spoke to each of the kids when they arrived and told the bigger ones to sit wherever they had sat last year. I put all the little ones on the first row and after I rang my old hand held bell to make it official, I began the task of learning about these 15 children I was to spend eight months with.

The surprises—along with the beginning of my own Ozark education—began right away.

"First off," I told them, "I'm Mr. Jayne and this is my first time ever teaching school. However, I know what I'm <u>supposed</u> to do and so do you older kids, so that's what we'll all go by."

Fifteen pairs of eyes looked me over with the most curiosity I had ever seen, none of it hostile or frightened or the least bit intimidated, only thorough. It was like children looking at a magician who may make a rabbit pop out of his hat. Or may not.

"Now, starting with our first graders, I want to get acquainted with everybody and then we'll get the seats sorted out." I pointed at one of the first graders, a little girl all dressed up for her first day of school in a clean pinafore, shiny pigtails, and shiny plastic shoes.

I asked her if she'd tell me her name and when I was sure I had it right, Glenda Faye, I asked her what her folks names were and what her daddy did for a living. She knew her parents names fine, but when it came to occupation, she thought about it and said, "He principally farms."

Now that stunned me. I had never heard many people use the word principally except school teachers, but here it was out of the mouth of a six year old who had, so far anyway, never spent a day in school. I scribbled a note on a back page of my notebook;

'principally — Glenda Faye.'

But this child wasn't done with me. She'd gotten to where she trusted my motives, I guess, and thought I deserved more. "But when he ain't farmin'," she added, "he mostly sets on the porch and plays the fiddle to beguile the time."

Beguile? Beguile the time? I couldn't believe my ears. Except for poetry or Shakespeare, I'd never heard any one use the word beguile in my 21 years and here was a child using it as comfortably as an Elizabethan courtier.

Before the day was over, I was going to find out that what I had heard was just the tip of an iceberg that had underlaid the Ozarks for nearly 300 years. I don't have my notes for that day anymore, but I don't need them. Let me recreate for you a few of the other archaic words they flung around in daily speech and which I had noted secretly so that I wouldn't embarrass them:

12 Noon: They called it "dinner," not lunch. One of my children was amazed at the size of the sack lunch my wife had fixed for me. He said, "Mamma packs us a big dinner but she don't ever pack sich a bait as that."

Also Noon recess: Broke up my first fight-thought it was the biggest boy Palmer Smith, (fourth grade) who started it. Billy, a third grader was stuck to him like a cocklebur. Palmer said, "I never started it, he beset upon ME." Billy said, "Well, I had to Mr. Jayne, he vilified my Pa." Then came Billy's big sister, May, to his defense: "Tain't right to bemean someone else's folks," she told me. The fight started because their "breachy" cow got into the Smith's strawberry patch and what wasn't "et" was "benastied." I'm not sure about vilified but I know what benasty means. After school: I asked Buck Ruther if he could

stay a few minutes "after books" and help
me reinforce the stovepipe. He said, (so help
me God,) "I'll come early in the morning,
Mr. Jayne, but now I best haste home.
Mamma don't sanction us bein' dilatory."

That was all in the first day. As days and weeks went
by, girls and boys began to open up to me about their
home life and families, and hardly a day went by that I
didn't scribble a word—new to me but old beyond belief—in my notebook for my own education. Sometimes
I wasn't sure whether I was teaching more to them or
learning more from them.

I was fond of all these children and wanted to give
them the very best education I could. What I was uneasy about was in doing so I would be required to replace their obsolete but beautiful language with one that
would work for them; they would be better at reading,
learning, and eventually learning a profession of some
kind. At the very least, I had to do something about
words that would get them laughed at anywhere outside of the Ozarks. For example, their pronunciation of
any word ending in *st*. To my students nests were nest-
es, posts were postes and floor joists were called jystes.
This odd addition of an extra 'es' sound was even added to wasps, which for some reason came out 'wastes'
and desks, which came out as 'deskes'. These words
were so natural they were hard to fix in school, because

all the kid's parents used them. I was introduced to one of the kid's uncles at a school "doin's" whose name, he said was "Noey," after the old feller that put all the beastes in the ark."

I really didn't want to change the children's way of seeing things or the beauty of words they used to describe what they saw and it was obvious that the teachers before me hadn't either. Most of their previous teachers had been from the Ozarks too. If one of these had heard a child say, "It sure takes an abundance of ten's to comprise a thousand." It would have probably sounded right to him or her just as wonderful words such as, "beguile," "dilatory," and "countenance". The last word, used as a verb, had been out of style since George III, the old fool who pushed the American colonies into Revolution. I also heard a fifth grader tell me his mother wouldn't "countenance either throwin' cards or blackguarding" in her house and knew that meant she wouldn't put up with them.

That first school term at Cross School was the beginning of my lifelong interest in the Ozark way of saying and looking at things. It would also be the last year for Cross School in that poor "deestrict." One of the families, with the most children, moved away and there were no longer enough students to pay a teacher. Six months after I taught the last class the old school house was sold, stripped of its desks and stove, then filled with hay. The days of the one room school were numbered.

I found another school and kept on teaching because I liked doing it and because I was determined to learn as much as I could about this stately speech before they consolidated all these little places. I knew only too well that when you put 30 kids in the same grade in the same room, they absorb each other's language like blotters. What I didn't realize was the lead mines would soon open in the Ozarks and people from other parts of the country would come in with their own ways of talking. It would become far more destructive than I could imagine. The infant television would soon be on its way into every mountain cabin and "Mother Tongue" in the mouths of children was doomed.

I learned about "Mother Tongue" from one of my wife's cousins, who had also taught school. She didn't know where the Middle English speech came from, she only knew it was a language children had inherited from people who had little commerce with modern speech and liked their own better.

I've told all I need to about one room schools and why I became an Ozarkian. Around those old school houses and the communities that used them, I met the people I would know for a lifetime; at coon hunts and fox meets, pie suppers and music making, turkey shoots, and around the smoke of deer camp fires. I would make friends with old men who still tell stories the same way and in the same words.

Just last year I heard one of my friends commenting on the believability of Dan Rather's news reporting,

"Now boys," he said, "that's the word with the bark on it!" I'm glad a few old timers still talk that way and I can't wait to tell you about the ones I have listened to.

The schoolhouses are mostly gone now and the few standing are falling-in on themselves for lack of children. Their windows cracked black spaces, their little rusty merry-go-rounds caught up and stopped in fists of briars. But before I go running on about them any more, all this talking about them has done one thing, it's reminded me of a story. . . .

*O*ne of my neighbors, who all the kids called Miz Bertha, was also a school teacher and she told me a story about one room schools and privies and what happened on one of her first days at school.

"I had three or four first graders that year," she said, "who of course had never been to school and I explained about the privies. 'Go out the door, boys turn right, girls turn left and the privies are at each side. If you have trouble with the latch on those old doors,' I told them, 'you can have one of the older children go with you the first time and show you, but I expect you to go by yourself after that.'

"Well of course I got busy passing out books and assigning seats and about the time I got them all settled where they belonged, I noticed the little Crocker boy in the first grade had his

hand up, and when I asked him what he needed, he whispered, 'I've got to go outside.' My,
that startled me, for he was just a little bitty feller
but he had a voice like a fog horn.

"So out the door he went and I don't know
how long he was gone, but I looked up and saw
him standing inside the door with his hand up,
waving it again. I said, 'Yes, Tommy, what is
it?' and he said, 'I can't find it.' He meant it as a
whisper, I reckon, but my land it carried like a
bullfrog and I had to hush some tittering.

"I said, 'Well, now, Tommy, you're in school
and I know you know your right from your left.
You go out the door, turn right and go back
along the schoolhouse. You can do it, you're a
big boy.'

"I couldn't believe it! That boy was back in less than a minute and he came right up to the desk this time. 'I CAN'T FIND IT!' he said, and I could see by the look on his face he was about panicked. I felt so sorry for him and told one of my eighth grader's, 'Lester, take Tommy out and show him where it is.'

"In a minute here came Lester back and he was laughing so hard it was all he could do to talk. I said, 'Lester Thompson—not thinking, you know—do you want to tell us what's so funny?'

"And he said, 'Miz Bertha, it wasn't the outhouse he couldn't find—his big sister dressed him for school and she put his britches on backwards!' "

Ozark Words

Careen (pronounced *kreen*)
To wear unevenly -or- tilt —
> "*No point buying that boy new shoes he'll have 'em careened in a week.*"

Comprise *To make up a given amount —*
> "*I don't know what they l'arn 'em now, but in my day two and two comprised four.*"

Conceit *To behave egotistically, To imagine superiority —*
> "*He conceits he's the best turkey caller around.*"

Confidence *Believe, have confidence in —*
> "*He claims it'll rain but I don't confidence that none.*"

Conjure *To think up -or- make up —*
> "*Since they got that car, all they do is set around and conjure up someplace to go.*"

Countenance *To put up with, to allow —*
> "*Mother never would countenance thowin' cards or cussin' around the house.*"

Cute *Clever, acute —*
> "*Now that bark peelin' machinery is pretty cute.*"

Chapter Three

PITCHERS DRAWED BY MITCH HISSELF

-Radio-
Second Dead Limb
Up In A White Oak Tree

I taught my last one room school in 1954 and at the close of the school year took a job at Salem, Missouri's radio station KSMO. Since my profession was going to be writing, it didn't seem to me that what I did to actually make a daily living would matter that much, and over the years it's proved to be true. As far as I know, nobody ever started out writing for a living. It's one of those things you have to work your way into, like being a fishing guide or maybe a congressman.

I found that being a radio announcer was a straight-forward occupation, demanding only that you speak reasonably good English, show up on time, and put your mind to work instead of your muscles. You had to learn to speak clearly and be really careful with time, but those were things that teaching a one room school had prepared me for already.

I realized, as time went by, that teaching had prepared me to be entertaining. The radio audience might be bigger, but like my students, they were all people waiting to hear what I would say next. I worked at it and developed a style that seemed to suit people. In a way it was the easiest work I had ever done, since my 'scholars' and their parents had already taught me how to talk comfortably to Ozark people.

I had learned a lot about Ozark customs and values, sayings and superstitions. I knew that "a whistling girl and a crowing hen will always come to some bad end," and I knew enough not to look at a new moon over my left shoulder. I had learned about weather signs and planting signs, and knew to keep the wind in my face while deer hunting, and how to call like a barred owl to get a turkey gobbler to answer back. I knew how to set traps and call in a coyote, how to listen to coon hounds and tell when they were "looking up" on a tree. I had learned that "when the wind is in the East, then the fishes bite the least," and that yellow jacket wasps are worse than hornets that would "fly up to roost of a evening," while yellow jackets will tackle you day or night. Best of all I had learned that music in the Ozarks was something you made yourself and was a family thing, as ordinary as cornbread. Everybody played something.

All in all I decided that I could probably entertain my neighbors as well as anybody else on the radio and after a year of learning how to use all the equipment, I started my own show. Our little station had 250 watts and barely sent its signal to the county line. There were lots of these 250 watters back then, scattered across Missouri and sounding as alike as cows. I decided that if KSMO couldn't be bigger it ought to be different, so instead of playing Nashville country music like all the rest, I played bluegrass, which after all, was played with the instruments most of my listeners kept under their beds or hanging on their walls. Bluegrass was mountain music; banjo, guitar, mandolin, and a fiddle if you had it.

Hickory Holler Time, which is what I called my show, lasted for nine years airing five days a week. When I look back, it was the funniest, most outrageous kind of radio. I told stories, dragged people in off the streets to take part in skits, made up stories about my sponsors, invented characters—like Zeke Dooley—to interview, and managed at one time or another to use the names of everybody I had ever met in my years of living in Dent County.

Let me interrupt myself right here with a Zeke Dooley story so you can sort of see what *he* was all about. Zeke was an ornery old hillbilly who didn't trust progress of any kind. Since I worked alone I had to use my own voice as the interviewer and do a different voice for Zeke, who was a slow talking old fellow without teeth. It was so hard to change voices that I ended up doing my Zeke stories on tape, but he was such a funny, aggravating old man and so Ozarkian that everybody liked him, and it was worth the trouble. I still do magazine stories, some 50 years later, using the old man to make a point. Zeke could get away with anything.

> **Mitch:** Today I'm visiting Zeke Dooley, Ozark Mountaineer, to talk about his career in making moonshine whiskey, a fast disappearing art in my part of the country.
>
> Zeke, I understand you call your product 'Cold Remedy.' What all goes into this 'Cold Remedy' of yours?
>
> **Zeke:** Corn, sugar, sorghum molasses, time and tender lovin' keer.
>
> **Mitch:** Do you have to have a lot of help?
>
> **Zeke:** Well, the wife, Perletta, she mostly does the wormern's work that don't take no expertise, like choppin' wood, keepin' the fire mended and shellin' corn.

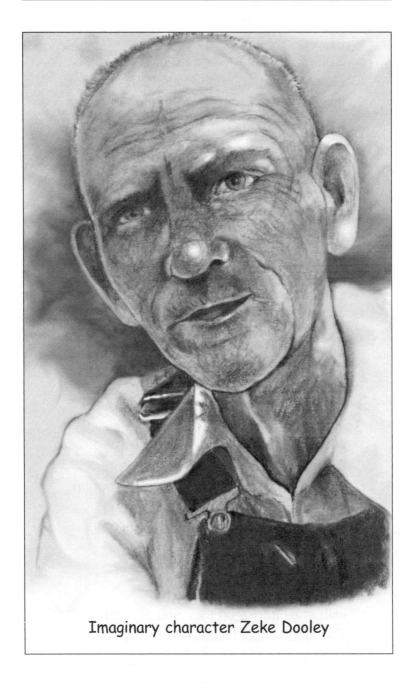

Imaginary character Zeke Dooley

Mitch: Women's work, huh?

Zeke: Not that wormern cain't do it all. I knowed a man had two daughters and them and their mother done the whole works, start to finish. What they call big wooly gals.

Mitch: Big wooly girls?

Zeke: Well, the kind of gals when they'd lift up an arm, two bats and a whippoorwill'd fly out. They could outwork three sawmill hands. Them girls growed hair on their back and got tattoos and developed big arm muscles so's they could favor their Ma.

Mitch: Big girls, I guess.

Zeke: Been any bigger a feller'd take a look and say, "Ship 'em!" Course they was jist makin' common moonshine—no finer work. Jist wrassle it into the jar.

Mitch: Your 'remedy' is more refined.

Zeke: Oh mercy yes. You take your average homemade likker, hit's all right if you was to want to git so drunk you have to hang onto the grass to lean agin' the ground.

Mitch: That strong, huh?

Zeke: I've knowed folks to wake up with snail tracks on their suit of clothes. The Dooley Cold Remedy is a-ways

more genteel. You jist sip along casual,
until the hide on your forehead feels
thick, knowin' you've worlds of time to
pick a soft place to land.
Mitch: You age the product, I suppose?
Zeke: Why that's the part I'm knowed
for. It has to age and meller fer thirty
days before my mark goes on it.
Mitch: And what is your mark?
Zeke: An 'X'.
Mitch: Which stands for?
Zeke: Dooley's Own Slow Cooked,
Double Twisted, Bottled In Barn Silo-
Scalin' Home Remedy.
Mitch: All that in an 'X'?
Zeke: Most of my customers cain't
read.

Whenever possible I brought in real people off the
streets of Salem to play or sing, or tell some ridiculous
story. I also would tell a story or two, crediting it to a
really unlikely source, such as some strait-laced banker
or merchant. Nobody knew when I would use their
name in vain and consequently everybody listened in
self defense. It was the most fun of anything I had yet
tried, and more than made up for the fact that I wasn't
teaching one room schools anymore. I still kept my old
notebook handy though, because now I had children's

parents listening to me and calling in with words I could add to my list; "I heerd it norated that they's a snow comin'. Any truth to that?"

I got double satisfaction from these calls. I got to look up words like 'norated' in my Oxford dictionary, and at the same time, got proof that unlike the theory of evolution, which nobody was buying, the older folks were ready to believe that the ex-schoolmaster had credibility when he gave the weather.

I made up a market report, called the *Dent County Tick and Snake Report* that was to become *Hickory Holler's* best known feature. It gave snake prices, "rattlers are shaky this morning"—egg prices, "buzzard eggs a dime, with buzzards in them, five cents"—tick prices, "Dry Valley White Dot Crush-Proof Wonders hanging on at twenty-five cents a bushel, stocker and feeder dog ticks steady at two cents, a few prime black hardback heifers with seed ticks by side bringing a dime," and listed all sorts of other Ozark products, like dressed snake sides, deer antlers, and tick bellies. I changed the prices faithfully every day and even had a make believe sponsor, Hoo Boy Tick Feeds—"If you don't say 'HOO BOY!' you haven't got a tick"—which also distributed Chigger Chunks and Snake Nuggets.

One of the things I had always liked the most about radio was the vivid, larger-than-life quality of the characters you could invent for it. Sound was everything and you could invent spoiled, whiny kids, blustering men, strident farm wives, all with the change in one person's vocal tone. You left the rest to the listener's imagination, which was probably as good as yours. Using old radio shows like *The Lone Ranger*, *Fibber McGee and Molly*, *Lum and Abner* for models, I constructed a different skit nearly every day for *Hickory Holler Time*. My favorite of these was "The Crump Family Saga" that I based on a local tribe of hillbillies who actually lived at the Salem dump in those days and made a living scavenging.

The real family was hilarious enough, since they had burrowed their way into an ancient saw dust pile, and lived in a warren of hollowed-out rooms shored up by scrap lumber and old car body parts. The patriarch of the clan was a scabrous looking old outfit who carried a garbage can slung from a leather strap and led his wife and ragtag kids in a charge on every fresh dumping of local trash, little of which ever touched the ground until it had been sorted and combed through. Since all Salem people hauled their own trash to the dump, we were all used to this startling family appearing like locusts before a person could get the tailgate down, or the trunk open, and we locals had nicknames for most of the kids. For strangers or tourists using the dump it could be considerably more traumatic seeing this bizarre family charging their vehicle; the old man in the lead with his twenty gallon garbage can, accompanied by his howling, enthusiastic wife and children. Many people locked themselves in their cars and fled.

"The Crump Family Saga" took this absurdity even further, the children all being named for things found in the dump. The boys were named, Muscatel, Prince Albert, Phlem—the emotional one—and Budweiser. The girls were, among others, Pudenda Lou, Davonette, the twins, Crayola and Victrola and little Cosmoline.

Peopled by whoever I could grab at the radio station, plus voices I would provide myself, a typical *Hickory Holler* intro of that time would read like this:

ORGAN MUSIC THEME:
"In A Country Garden"
by Percy Granger
ANNOUNCER VOICE OVER:
And once again we invite you to join us as we visit that happy-go-lucky family we all know, The Crumps at the Dump. Today our little family of hopeful scavengers gathers around the breakfast table—which is the hood of a 49 Ford—to plan the day's activities. Let's listen in . . . .
PA CRUMP: All right kids, pass your license plates for some of Ma's great

oatmeal. (SOUND EFFECTS: metal clashing) And remember it's Pudenda Lou's turn to use the spoon today.

PUDENDA: Oh goody!

MA CRUMP: Now is everybody here? Muscatel, it's your turn to keep track of the children.

MUSCATEL: All present and can count to four.

MA CRUMP: That's accounted for son. Where's Prince Albert?

MUSCATEL: He was here a minute ago. Where's Prince Albert, Crayola? You guys were playing with your pet flies.

CRAYOLA: Maybe the bathroom fell in on him again. You know Prince Albert is always in the can. (giggles)

MA CRUMP: No jokes young lady. Go check will you Phlem?

PHLEM: Gollee, Mom, it's always me that has to go dig him out. (Distant SOUND EFFECTS: digging around in debris) Here he is! A fender fell on him. You all right, Prince Albert?

PRINCE A: (crying) I lost my fly! My real pretty green'un.

MA CRUMP: That's all right, we'll get you another one. Pa, you are going to have to do something about that bathroom ceiling. Somebody's going to get hurt.

PA CRUMP: All right Ma, I'll dig another one today. (SOUND EFFECTS OF A TON OF JUNK FALLING)

MA CRUMP: Now who can that be, this early? And me with my hair up!

PA CRUMP: All right children, it's an early delivery! Muscatel, you're on hub caps today, Victrola, you're on bottles, who's on cans?

(CHORUS OF VOICES) Me! Me! No, ME! (Etc.)

PA CRUMP: (firmly) Now children, be fair, I think it's Davonette's turn. Pudenda Lou, you take boxes and Cosmoline will be in charge of used food.

(EXCITED CHATTER AND CLATTERING SOUND EFFECTS AS FAMILY GETS READY)

MA CRUMP: (BANGING ON PAN TO GET EVERYONE'S ATTENTION) Now remember, kids, everybody meet at the wrecked Studebaker at two

o'clock sharp! Dad's going to hook the
battery up, and what are we going to
listen to?
(EVERYBODY YELLS) Hickory Holler
Time! (MUSIC UP —"FLINT HILL
SPECIAL")

Radio was a great way to get to know people. Listeners got to recognize my voice, accept me and even trust me after a while. After all, I was the person who brought them weather, and news, and told them which creeks were impassable during a storm. I told them who was in the hospital, who had been in an auto accident, and who had died. I warned them if a tornado was coming, and told them whether the school busses would run if it was snowing. What a way to collect an audience, in case you needed one, and I had already decided that I was a performer of sorts. Teaching school was performing and even writing was a kind of performance demanding readers. Radio was good theater even if the audience was invisible. I set the stage every day.

"This is colorful KSMO, friends," I told them, "250 watts of pulsating, penetrating power, coming to you from our palatial suite of glassed-in, wall to wall carpeted, tastefully decorated and guaranteed 100% bat proof studios, second dead limb up on the west side of a white oak tree in the head of Salem's own *Hickory Holler*." All this to introduce a two hour Bluegrass music and comedy show on a little one-horse station, but it worked. To my own surprise the show was soon completely sponsored by the very people I'd hoped would support it. These were unusual sponsors to fit an unusual program, a harness and leather shop, a shade tree auto repair shop, and a junk yard to begin with. Then there were more established places; a little grocery store, a car dealer, a bank, and a liquor store. Before long I had all the sponsors I needed.

As one of my sponsors told a friend, "Of course the son-of-a-bitch is crazy, but people come in to say, 'did you hear what Mitch Jayne said about you?' and then they buy something."

Hickory Holler, as much as it did for my creativity and as hard as I worked to write those shows, wasn't the part of radio that was to change my life. Saturday morning radio was what did that.

On Saturday mornings I was the board engineer for Howe Teague's radio program, *Howe Teague and The Gang* on KSMO. Back in those old days the local talents around towns like Salem came in to play live in the studios of the local radio stations and on programs like Howe Teague's. This was the custom all over the South half of the country. These were mostly country music bands doing the songs they had learned from records or the Grand Ol' Opry radio broadcasts. Most of the bands around Salem played on the weekend and were sponsored by the bar or roadhouse where they were to appear. The bands were almost uniformly awful since music was just a weekend thing and nobody worked at it. The exception to this was *Howe Teague and The Gang*, an old mountain music band that only played for family

Storyteller Howe Teague

type events like pie suppers, square dances and the like. Howe Teague was an old time fiddler and though his band varied from time to time on his Saturday morning radio show, he never did, sawing off old square dance tunes and waltzes and introducing whoever showed up, with his own wit and down-home humor.

Howe Teague and I became friends and I was fascinated with his ability to tell stories and jokes—always about local people—and interweave them with the music. It was pretty much what I did on *Hickory Holler Time* and gave us a lot in common. I began going out to his log cabin on weekends to visit and sit in on fox hunts with him and his neighbors. Howe was no ordinary storyteller and I studied his way of telling a joke, the way he built on it until I would understand the nature of the person the joke was on. Howe never told regular punch line jokes, his were funny stories about people he knew.

Here is one he told on Glenn Capps who owned Salem's only music store and tuned pianos for people. I might as well tell that one and try to tell it like Howe told it. . . .

"Well now, you know, Joe Capps, that was Glenn's daddy, went to buy himself a truck one time, this was back in the thirties, and Joe, he'd never had one. Never had learned to drive, you know, lot of people didn't back then. So Joe agreed to buy Glen Stayton's old truck if Stayton would teach him how to drive it. So they got out in an old field, where he wouldn't run into nothing and Joe got behind the wheel with that Stayton feller showin' him what to do.

"Now, Glenn, he wasn't but maybe ten years old, he wanted in on that y'see, and he clambered up into the stake bed. Kept his hands in his pockets because it was a cold day, and leaned up ag'inst the cab to where he could hear what Stayton was tellin' his dad. . . wanted to learn how to drive it himself, y'know.

"Well old Joe, he had his jaw set and he was taking it serious, you see, he wasn't studyin' where Glenn was. He revved her up and lets out the clutch and that truck tuck off and jist walked Glenn right off the end of it. But before he could fall, Joe mashed on the brakes, and here he come back up with his hands still stuck down in his pockets and slammed into the stock rack. Well now, that went on fer maybe a minute, whippin' that lad ag'inst the front and nearly dumping him off the back, because Joe, he hadn't no idee his boy was back there— he was taken up with working those gears.

44

It was the most comical thing to watch you ever saw, Joe just frailin' that big looby boy back and forth, and him with his hands still in his pockets.

"Well, after a while Joe got stopped and Glenn, he finally managed to get his hands out of his pockets and jumped off that truck bed. One of the neighbors was there watchin' the whole thing and he says, 'Glenn, why didn't you get off of that truck when you had a chance?' and Glenn, he kindy hung his head, embarrassed you know, and he says, 'Now what chance was that?' "

Howe had worked for the county highway crew for nearly thirty years and his stories were centered on the very types of Ozark people I had come to the Ozarks to learn about.

Here's one I remember. . . .

"Now that puts me in mind of Snuffy Dougherty, you lookin' at your watch like that. Did I ever tell you about him? Well, Snuffy— you know we called him that because he looked just like that Snuffy Smith in the comics feller— anyway, he got him a watch one time, one of those big old Sears Roebuck railroad watches. Big around as a jar lid and pretty near as thick, and he was proud of that watch, you know. Kept a-pullin' it out of his bib pocket to look it over like it was the newest invention man had come up with. Paid a dollar for it, I expect, and wanted us to know he had it. Well, we was clubbin' weeds, out on the right-of-way in that hot sun, and Snuffy would dip into his bibs every little while and look at his watch. That got to ticklin' everybody, you know, but we never let on. Finally, John Miller, he was foreman back then, he decided to have some fun out of Snuffy and he says, 'Snuffy, what time of day is it?' and Snuffy he hauled out his watch and studied it and says, 'Well now, this here

watch of mine says it's 3:15, John. But I'm not sure that's right, I just set it by a cheap little old radio we got at the house.' "

Now that was a Howe Teague story, full of local color and based on something ridiculous.

What I learned from Howe Teague about story-telling was that a storyteller's style and descriptive terms were more important than the outcome or "payoff line." The word pictures were everything and a listener laughed with Howe, when he told of a woman "built kindly like a meat loaf," or a man who had no teeth, who when he laughed, "just held his mouth wide, like a big pink square and you could see that little guinea horn a-hangin' down." You could 'see' whatever Howe told about.

Howe's stories described people, not in detail but just enough for you to form your own mental picture, sort of the way I had to do things on the radio. I had always liked the way radio allowed you to form your own pictures and I worked for that familiarity you always got from *Fibber McGee and Molly*, *Fred Allen* and *Lum and Abner*. If the storyteller gave you the right clue, you could provide the visual things to make the story funny. Take this story, for instance, that Howe told me years ago, which was the kind of thing you could tell on the radio.

"Lookin' at that cat there reminds me of one we used to have back when I was growin' up. Dad always told a story on that cat. It always stayed around the barn but in bad weather or a big snow it would come  up the house and we'd let it in for a while—feed it a little. Come time to turn it out, that cat would allus head for a big white oak tree we

 had in the yard, because the hounds were bad to get after it. It would stand in the doorway long as it could, kindy peering round for them and then make a break for that tree. Here would come them hounds a-boilin' out from under the house and rare up on that tree baying.

"Well, one year light-  ning killed that tree and Dad had to cut it down, afraid it would fall and get on the house, you know. And next time it came a big snow that cat came up to spend the day, and when Dad put it out, all the hounds was in the yard waitin' to be fed. That cat lit out for the white oak like he allus did and Dad claimed it run thirty feet straight up in the air before it seen that tree was gone!"

Country folks, who all had cats, loved to hear that one and he had a dozen like it dealing with things and people that everybody recognized.

Howe wanted me to come along with him to pie suppers and maybe act as auctioneer. He said that I ought to learn to play an instrument and I could go as part of the band. I told him that if I could get someone to teach me how to play the banjo I'd really like to go and meet all the people he knew.

I had already met a lot of musicians on Howe's radio show and particularly liked a couple of boys who came in to play on the program, The Dillard brothers, Doug and Rodney. Douglas was a wonderful banjo picker and his brother played everything. I couldn't ask Douglas to teach me anything. He worked in St. Louis and was only home occasionally, and besides was way too good at his three-finger Scruggs style to fool with frailing, which is the old-time style I wanted to learn. His brother Rodney, however, offered to teach me, in exchange for a .22 pistol and one of the hounds I was always swapping for.

Meeting Rodney was a Godsend. Not only was he a good banjo teacher but he knew more about Bluegrass than anyone I had ever met. He helped me pick records for *Hickory Holler Time* and loaned me some from his collection. I learned enough about a banjo from him to tune it and play enough songs to 'second' behind Howe's fiddle tunes; old timers like *Ragtime Annie, Rye Straw, White River,* and *Cluck Old Hen.* 'Seconding' was the old time word for rhythm accompaniment, and all I had to do was watch the guitar player, listen to the bass and keep time. Within a month I was going along with

Howe to square dances, thanks to Rodney's banjo lessons. I'd always had a good ear for harmony and pitch so I could even sing a little bass on the songs, but mainly my function was to just hammer away on the banjo and say something between songs.

Howe Teague was a superb square dance fiddler and as tireless as any fiddler I ever heard, laying the tune down for eight sets of clattering feet that kept far better time than

Teenager Rodney Dillard

I could. In between sets we would go outside, swap stories, and drink from offered bottles of whatever the men had brought. We drank moonshine if it was handy and I got to make the acquaintance of several old time moonshiners, finally meeting one who invited me to come see how it was made. That man was the inspiration for the 'Zeke Dooley' character I was to get so much mileage out of over the years.

"Now this here is the pure quill," he told me, "and you kin drink it from the coil, need be. I don't make no second handed whiskey." He was as proud of his skill as any old craftsman, having learned it from his father. I could tell he was pleased that it was illegal and that element adds that 'Zeke' flavor to a lot of Ozark stuff, like hunting deer with hounds or killing one when you need meat rather than observing the season. "When they's a discrepancy between a made law and a natchr'l law," he said once after we'd become friends, "I'm partial to nature. I don't set my table by city folk's rules."

I was learning everything I could about the people who were my neighbors and I wanted to get it right. The thing was, I had begun by wanting to be able to write about the Ozark way of life but from the first day I had come to this part of Missouri I had ceased being objective. I no longer looked at Dent County as someplace to write about. I had felt, coming here, a deja-vu, a sense that I had been here before in another life and I wanted to live that life again.

None of this stopped me from writing—far from it. I was beginning to sell stories to a lot of different magazines and had even written a book about what I had learned from the woods, called *Forest In The Wind*. It didn't sell all that well but at least I could say I was a writer in case anybody asked me. Not too many people did, because I had become one of them by then; an Ozark man whose job was in radio.

D Ozark Words

Dauncy Finicky, particular, feeling uneasy —
"He was snake bit last week and he's still dauncy about his vittles."

Deef Deaf —
"He's so deef he cain't hear hisself fart."

Denote Indicate —
"When whippoorwills shuts up before midnight, that denotes rain before day."

Dilatory Tardy or lax —
"Oh, Sam's good fer his credit, but he'll be dilatory about payin' on time."

Discomfit Embarrass or discomfort —
"I'll take cream in my coffee if it won't discomfit ye none."

Disfurnish Take away a needed thing —
"I'd be obliged to borry your mule if it wouldn't disfurnish ye."

Disremember Forget —
"I've seen that feller, but I disremember his name."

Docile (pronounced Doe-cile) Tame, easily controlled —
"His last wife was a docile critter but this one ain't."

Dornick (pronounced Donnick) A rock —
"You could put that boy to mowin' a ball park and he'd find a big donnick to bust the blade on."

Chapter Four

"You boys are sure going a long way to flop!"

By the year 1962 I was chief announcer at KSMO, whatever that meant. I had been there longer than anyone except the owner and I was making $100 a week, which was considered top dollars. My title was in lieu of money, of which KSMO was always short. I had been offered a job at KMOX in St. Louis for a bigger salary, but somehow a career in radio wasn't what I saw for myself. I knew that the biggest talent I had shown so far was in telling backwoods stories and I didn't think big city radio was going to be a place to use what I did best. I knew I had to get out of Salem and do something, because I had two very bright children who were growing up fast and someday might want to broaden their horizons and maybe go to college.

One of the things that made me decide to look for an alternative to spending the next twenty years at home was a letter I got from an airline pilot.

He said, "I fly over the Ozarks from St. Louis to Dallas-Ft. Worth three times a week and my Second Officer and I like hillbilly music. I found your station a while back and realized that with a little 'doctoring' of our course I could listen to the *Tick and Snake Market Report*. We got such a kick out of it we decided to share it with the passengers so they could know what kind of people they were flying over. I thought you'd like to know that you now have a daily audience of 200 or so people flying over you at 3 o'clock. Keep up the funny stuff."

He asked me not to tell his name or the airline's, and I never did. I only made reference to people, "passing through" when I gave the tick market, and added, "some of them 20,000 feet up—look out for Frankie Schwartz." This last was a tribute to one of my sponsors who owned a junk yard and built his own airplane out of spare parts, flying it to Vichy, Missouri, for his flying lessons

Frankie was a wonderful man who
often wrecked his plane and then
came on the radio to cover his own
crash on our local news programs.
Frankie always claimed that God was
his copilot, which made most of us
wonder where God took *his* flying lessons.

The airline pilot's letter got me
to thinking; what was funny to
Dent County might be funny to a
lot of people elsewhere. I was 33 years
old and still young enough to make a career change.

What persuaded me to leave KSMO, however, was
knowing the Dillard brothers who had decided to have
a try at show business. They had already gone to a studio
in St. Louis and recorded a single record and it had fired-
up their blood. Together, with their friend Dean Webb,
Rodney and Douglas had been hanging out at my house
a lot to rehearse things they might do on stage. I kept
coming up with funny ways to introduce songs and what
to say about my three friends. As time went by, it was
easier to imagine myself as part of their act, a sort of
Ozark spokesman. The problem with that line of thinking
was I didn't play an instrument they could use. I sure
didn't want to stand around with a tambourine or a Jew's
harp looking like 'Ned in the third reader,' as my aunt
used to say, while these red-hot musicians were picking.

A young Dean Webb

Dean Webb, who had played bass for a band, still had his bass fiddle and that took care of that objection. He volunteered to teach me how to play it. By late summer of 1962 I could play about ten songs passably with my three friends teaching me about Bluegrass timing, showing me licks, and lecturing me on harmony so I could sing bass on songs. Because I was so enthusiastic about what we were going to do I learned very quickly. I had also started writing songs with Dean and Rodney. I wanted to be of value to this group of incredible pickers and not feel like an impostor. I wrote a song with Dean, called *The Old Home Place*, while we were on the back porch of my house, and *I'll Never See My Home Again* with Rodney. Both songs were about missing what I hadn't even left yet.

We planned on taking the music to the West coast, preparing for the trip like we were a wagon train heading west, taking just the barest of necessities. All of us knew better than to go to Nashville, which had never loved Bluegrass all that much anyway, so we pointed Dean's old automobile toward California.

Rodney and Doug's Aunt Dollie's parting words, and I expect she spoke for everyone were, "You boys are sure going a long way to flop!" Meaning that it would be more thrifty to flop someplace closer to the house. What nobody at home knew was just how good the Dillards were. We didn't know either, but we intended to find out.

Our first stop was Oklahoma City, where our money ran out and we had to work at various day jobs until a local folk music club, 'The Buddhi,' finally hired us to play for a week. On stage I used every funny line I could think of and between songs told outlandish stories about home. One of my first introductions, which we were to use for years, was:

"Hi, we're The Dillards and we're all hillbillies. I thought I'd better tell you that, because I expect you thought we were the Budapest String Quartet. Actually, we all come from a little town in the Ozarks where moss grows on the north side of people."

That tongue-in-cheek presentation of who we were worked and so did we. We had decided the music, as good as it was, was going to need all the help it could get in Hollywood.

I don't believe anyone ever worked harder at making believers than we did with those first Oklahoma audiences. Every night found us totally exhausted but a lot smarter than when we went on stage. Rodney and I, who had all the funny lines, were learning timing and the mechanics of stage comedy. Rodney played the little brother of the family—he was just 19—and he was great at being the weird one. I introduced Rodney by saying: "And here is Rodney, who we have with us to remind you that every sixty-seconds, mental illness strikes. . . ."

Rodney had—and has—a wonderful plastic face that could look dumber than Spam and we used his ability to write skits around him, so it was like me playing Abbott to his Costello. The audience loved Rodney's musical-vegetable character, which we played in order for Rodney to always come out the winner in any argument or situation. He was the idiot-savant whose singing always gave the lie to his acting and made the comedy a spoof. Douglas, meanwhile, played his banjo with breakneck speed, grinning with the pleasure of picking for strangers. Dean while providing his own cleverness on the mandolin also had a great stone faced presence and he completed the characters we were selling.

Those Oklahoma audiences were great training for us. They loved stories about people back home, they consumed the music like they were starved and they packed 'The Buddhi' every night. Between our enthusiasm, high speed picking, and what I can only guess was our back-woods charm, we brought in enough people to be hired for another week. 'The Buddhi' had proved to us that we had the right idea. Bluegrass was wonderful music but what audiences wanted was to be entertained by it, not lectured. The Dillards were the only Bluegrass group those people had ever seen who had as much fun with who they were as what they did.

After Thanksgiving we were able to get on the road and head for Hollywood. We had $400 and the confidence we needed a lot more than the money. We knew that we were going to make good, we just weren't sure whether the folks back home were ever going to know about it. All I knew was I was writing and performing and for the first time I believed I was living up to whatever potential I might have outside of Dent County, Missouri. For better or worse, I was a member of something and no longer on my own.

There has been so much written about The Dillards that I don't want to clutter up a bunch of stories with a lot of biographical stuff about the group. I would like to mention, though, that we had a lot of help and encouragement along the way, and I'll never forget the day we finally pulled Dean's old Cadillac, and its one-wheel trailer, over to the curb in front of a motel on Melrose Avenue in Hollywood. We had survived the first part of the plan.

Green as we were it didn't matter in Los Angeles; no one cared what anyone looked like. It was the strangest mixture of weirdness and laid-back living we had ever seen, with every oddball in the country right in his own element.

That first night we drove down Sunset Boulevard, gaping out the windows like tourists and Dean spotted a Rolls Royce with Tennessee plates ahead of us.

"I bet that's Roy Acuff." He said, as excited as Dean ever got. "I'm gonna pull up and see if it is."

We came alongside and the driver looked over to see four rustics staring at him. He glanced at us amused, through his sunglasses, and said something to his passengers.

"Hell, it's just Elvis." Said Dean and we drove on. Every time I think of us in those days I remember that and laugh. Roy Acuff was about the highest caliber any of us could chamber in those days and we weren't aiming any higher.

What happened to us next was so far beyond what anyone at home would have ever expected of us. I still hesitate to write about it, I'm afraid some other quartet of fools will try it and all starve to death in a pile. It reminds me that one time I killed a running deer with one shot from a pistol and I knew it was just dumb luck. There are spaces in your life when plain dumb luck is just about everything.

The Dillards auditioned at a folk club called 'The Ash Grove,' just "bringing our music in," as they say back home, into the lobby of the club where the main act's record producer happened to listen to us. It was the most gauche and naive thing we could have done, but luck stayed with us. That's what eventually got us a record contract with Elektra Records at a time when most

Bluegrass pickers couldn't get arrested. The contract signing, when it happened, was duly noted in *Variety Magazine*. A first album was put into the planning stage, which like everything else with record companies, takes forever, but at least we could say we had an album in the works. The album was going to be called, *Back Porch Bluegrass.*

Meanwhile, we set in to work at every job we could get, no matter how small, auditioning for anyone who would listen. The word that we were new, funny and cheap spread around among owners of the dozen or so coffee houses and clubs who would take a chance on 'hillbilly' music. These club owners were stretching what turned out to be the last days of the folk revival. At that time there were performers like José Feliciano, Bud and Travis, Dan Hicks and His Hot Licks, comedy teams like Willard and Greco, The Smothers Brothers and single acts such as Steve Martin, Pat Paulsen, Roger Miller and Lily Tomlin. It was a bewildering field we'd entered and no one could figure out where Bluegrass belonged in it. We were funny as well as musical and that was our salvation, so we were beginning to attract fans that followed us from club to club.

61

This is one of the stories I would tell on stage to introduce songs:

Mitch: We had this man back home who was what you would call a professional drinker, meaning he would drink anything that hadn't gotten too stiff to pour. Ebo Walker was his name, and he'd warm up on things like Liquid Wrench, or tractor radiator alcohol. He'd made a name for himself testing moonshine and he had some status. He was kind of a role model for kids who had seen their own daddies throw-up their socks on Schlitz down at the Legion Hall and wanted to do better in life. Kids would walk up to Ebo at the pool hall and hand him a pint, say, "Ebo, I don't guess you'd want to try this stuff we made-up to take the grasshoppers off a windshield, would you?" And old Ebo, he'd just reach down, kind of dignified, and take what they had. Ebo was kind of like a wine taster, he'd roll it around in the jar and take a sip, say stuff like, "Well this here is explosive without being impertinent," or some such thing and drink it off. Of course he spent a lot of time down, drinking like that. He got so he'd recognize people by their ankles.

62

Well, Rodney and I made up a song about him and the reason we did was that he finally died. Of course a lot of people do that, but his way was kind of unusual. He died in the privy. . . . Now what happened, he'd keep a little horn of something out on the back porch to start his day, and he got up one winter morning, snow on the ground and went out to have his instant breakfast of Wynn's Friction Proofing or whatever it was, and went out to the privy.

Well, his wife wasn't too bright, you know—she didn't even know he drank— and about the third day she begun to get uneasy about him. Sent one of the bufords out to see what had happened to his dad and he came back and kid-like, just told it like he saw it. He said, "He's out there in the privy froze-up stiffer than a wood-pecker's lip." And sure enough he was. . . . Of course it was cold weather and he'd kept real good, but he had kind of setup in there, sitting down, you know . . . and it was hard to load him.

Rodney: They let him sit up in front of the hearse like anybody else. . . . Had his hand out the window, people thought he was waving. . . . Actually, he died reaching for the catalogue.

Mitch: Yeah, and the reason Rodney and I wanted to write this is it was kind of a landmark. They buried him there in the cemetery and when the thaw came, he killed the grass for 50 feet around—and resurrected a couple of Jehovah's Witnesses next plot over.

Aside from long stories such as that, I continued to try to make myself useful on stage. When someone would break a string it would give me a chance to light my pipe, lounge on my bass and tell a story, taking the audience's attention away from the dreary mechanical business of winding on a string and retuning. I had my work cut out for me since The Dillards were full of adrenaline and drive, and broke strings nearly every set.

My stories had to be just the right length or my partners would have to stand around and wait for me to finish. I got around that by throwing stories or lines, or tidbits like 'whittled words' that even the rest of the band had never heard, to keep them interested too. (Whittled words are homemade Ozark words and you'll find a bunch of them later in this book.)

None of us ever looked bored on stage and critics were always pleased with us, commenting that we seemed to entertain each other as well as the audience. My pipe was almost magical as a stage prop, giving us a relaxed, amiable look that no other Bluegrass band I'd ever watched seemed to have. The curling smoke from the pipe gave a nice touch to short bits and made them more real, like this little joke I used for filler when everybody had gotten out of tune and needed cover:

*W*hen school got out back home I had to make a living the other four months and I took to painting signs. I'd studied that a little in college and I could letter a mailbox or the side of a truck cab or whatever. Well, they had this hardware store back home, Dent Brothers, where you could buy anything from stovepipe to horseshoes and they had gotten in a big load of cast iron stuff, like sinks and bath tubs. They hired me to paint a sign to put out. So I was out on the sidewalk in front of the store lettering a big piece of plywood and this old man was watching me pretty close. Directly he said, "Now just what does that sign say? I left my glasses at the house."

Well, the letters were about a foot high, so I knew glasses weren't his problem, but I told him; "It says, CAST IRON SINKS." And he looked kind of disgusted and says, "Well, Goddamighty son, any fool knows that!"

It was gentle fun but our bits were a lot more insightful than other Bluegrass bands were doing and we were in demand. A few junior colleges even hired us to bring this 'primitive' music to the campus for purposes of education. Since there are more of these in Southern California than anything except maybe used car lots, these concerts helped us to bring an audience to the struggling clubs. Somehow we managed to make a living from one week to another.

It was early in 1963 when lightning struck. Dick Linke, Andy Griffith's manager, had remembered reading an item in *Variety* about Elektra signing some boys from the Ozarks and decided to apply it to a script that had been written for *The Andy Griffith Show* entitled, 'The Darlings Are Coming.' The script called for a family of mountain people who were musical, but otherwise outlandish, and headed by a strong rustic father figure who spoke for all of them. The man we had hired to manage us when we got the Elektra contract, called us excitedly. We were to report to Desilu Studios with our instruments and audition for Andy Griffith.

Of all the good things that could have happened to us, this was the ultimate good fortune. We arrived at Desilu and were brought onto a set as familiar, in a way, as our own home town. Everybody back home who had a television watched *The Andy Griffith Show* and in the summer of 1962 The Dillards interrupted our back porch rehearsals many a night to watch it. Andy Griffith was 'mountainy' and every little town in the Ozarks had a Barney Fife, an Otis Campbell, and a half dozen scurrying Aunt Bees. It was like a small miracle, being invited to audition for what was probably the only television show in Hollywood that could use what we did. . . and we had only been in town two months!

We entered the sound stage reverently and looked around at all the cluster of lights, the fixtures of motion picture making, and the Sheriff's office set we had seen so often.

Andy came out accompanied by Dick Linke, Aaron Rueben the producer, and Bob Sweeny who directed those shows, and we played for them. I introduced everybody, the way we did on stage and we played a couple of Doug's banjo tunes and Rodney sang *Dooley*, among other things, a song we had written about an old moonshiner. We didn't know what they were looking for, so we just did the best we could. I smoked my pipe as I always did, Douglas grinned at his work, like he always does, and Dean looked like a figure on Mt. Rushmore, as he's always done. I don't know what Rodney did, but I knew that Andy liked the way we all looked.

Andy was wonderful. He laughed and talked to us and asked us about the Ozarks. He was such a comfortable man and even made us part of a joke on Bob Sweeny, who asked innocently if we knew his favorite song, *The Big Rock Candy Mountain*. Andy winked at us and told Bob he was sure we would play it if he would sing it. The joke was that though Bob Sweeney had a lot of talents, singing wasn't one of them. He couldn't carry a tune on a snow shovel but it turned out that Andy never ceased encouraging him to try, to the great amusement of the cast and crew who were in on the gag. Of course, we weren't, and I was nervous because I didn't even remember how the song went. Rodney started the song out on the guitar and we soon realized what the joke was, Bob was tone deaf and couldn't anymore find a key and stick to it than a hound, but he kept trying until Andy was nearly on the floor with laughter. It was like Andy to get us comfortable with his sense of humor right away and make us feel like we were already part of something.

It was the way he did everything, and we were to learn he was one of those rare complete souls who aren't affected by the trappings of success. He always dealt with people one-on-one, was totally considerate, and always treated us as fellow professionals.

On that memorable day he told us that he liked our music, liked the way we looked, thought we were right for the part, and made us feel like we had the job. He invited us to sit in on a read-through of the script on the following Monday where he introduced us to our fellow actors; Denver Pyle, who would play our Pa, Briscoe Darling; Maggie Peterson, who would play our sister, Charlene; and Hoke Howell, who was to play Charlene's boyfriend, Dud Wash. Andy also took time to explain that once we had all agreed on some songs we would pre-record our music in order to get the best possible quality of sound.

This was the beginning of a relationship and a TV identity that was to last three years, from 1963 to 1966. The Darling family was used in six episodes during that time, which doesn't seem like a lot of exposure until you realize that the show has been in constant reruns ever since, making a total of more than 36 years our music has been played on television. We were hired as musicians rather than actors, thanks to Andy, and are still paid

ASCAP royalties from every show that's rerun long after the actors' residuals have run out. Andy had always urged us to use our own songs when they would work with the script, in order for us to get writers and composer's royalties as well.

We would be performing on the road sometimes and get word that Jim Fritzell and Everett Greehbaum, the two men who wrote a lot of the Griffith shows, had come up with another Darling family script. It didn't matter if we had been gone for a few months or a year, everybody on the set was glad to see us and work with us again. It was like coming back to a home base. Bob Saunders, the dour and all-business Assistant Director, even softened up for us and would kid us with things like, "this time you guys are all gonna be in drag. We're calling it, 'The

Darlings Go Lavender.' " or, "Hey, look who we got, the family that's cheaper'n an animal act." Earlier on Bob had told us shows that contained music or animals always cost the most to do, because they required so many takes, but we didn't. In Bob's dry way it was a compliment and he didn't give many of those.

If only for these things, I would always be thankful to Andy Griffith, but there was more to it than that. *The Andy Griffith Show* set was a 'happy set,' an old Hollywood maxim meaning that if the star is happy, the set is pleasant and the actors like their work. In all of the other television programs we were on later, I never saw a cast or crew as at ease and unfailingly civil, more liable to play practical jokes on each other, remember each other's birthdays or ante-up for a special occasion than *The Andy Griffith Show*. I couldn't help think it was because the show was such a gentle, good natured look at how humans could get along that it had to filter into the daily attitudes of the people working there.

In between takes, Don Knotts and Andy would go over their lines, cracking each other up with ad lib comments, or while waiting for the lights to be set, they would do things like throw darts, something at which Don excelled and Andy was mediocre. Andy would stand back to look at Don's score and shout, "Don, you hateful puke!" or, "I'm gonna whup you if it harelips the Pope." Andy was totally happy in his work and his big laugh was irresistible when something struck him funny. Very rarely Don would blow a line and when he did

Andy would pretend to make a production of it, "Looky here, I've had to memorize the Constitution and you ain't got but four little bitty lines and can't even say them straight?"

I don't think I have ever seen two actors who regarded each other as highly as those two. Both total pros who could work to each other's timing and crack each other up between takes.

Denver Pyle, our TV Pa, took The Dillards "to raise," as the expression goes, explaining the immensely boring waiting time that is 80 percent of an actor's day. None of us could believe the amount of time it took to set up the lights and camera movements for one piece of dialogue, as much as 40 minutes for a shot of Don and Andy doing a two minute exchange. They were using only one camera and there would be a set-up for a 'two shot' of the pair, then a set-up for a close-up of each face, with the lines being repeated for each camera position. It was Andy's decision to have the show filmed with only one camera and Denver explained that this would reflect a special 'feel' in the final cut. He explained "It's like the difference between hearing music and actually watching somebody play it." It made sense to us. Sitcoms that were shot with two or more cameras (to save time) didn't compare to the quality and intimacy of the one-camera filming of *The Andy Griffith Show*.

I think the "difference" is what still makes *The Andy Griffith Show* cast—for those of us who are still here—get together now and then for reunions; to let people see that we too, value that funny little town of memory. Andy doesn't take part in these and for good reason, I think. He is still creating jobs and challenges for himself and doesn't take time to rehash his past successes. For him I expect it would be like a movie star going back to a high school reunion to lord it over his friends, thereby diminishing what they had become. Andy doesn't do that kind of thing. He has no more personal vanity than a threshing machine. He simply likes to work at his craft. As he told us one time, when Dean innocently asked him why he didn't drive a Rolls Royce, "I don't like people lookin' at me when I'm not workin'."

By the time *The Andy Griffith Show* went off the air in 1968, The Dillards had established themselves as entertainers and we had plenty of work, but we too had undergone changes. Douglas had left the group, Rodney had decided on a new direction for his music, and I was getting deaf. The deafness, which is thought to be genetic, was scary, but my writing, which I had never slacked on during my career as a musician, was beginning to pay off. Together with Rodney and other Dillards I had co-written 40-some songs and made eight albums, which like books and stories, would always remain a testimony that I'd been here and done <u>something</u>.

The real evidence I might make a living at what I had started out to do at 18 was when I sold a book called, *Old Fish Hawk,* to Lippincott, which gave me the courage to take a part-time job with Dick Clark, writing for some of his shows in between Dillard jobs. I was trying to find a way to go home after 12 years and take up writing full time.

When *Old Fish Hawk* went into paperback with Pocketbooks, and was optioned by Twentieth Century Fox for a film, I got up my courage and said good-bye to my old friends The Dillards. I had been homesick for the Ozarks as long as I could bear it and was coming home to do what I was intended to do. Instead of writing songs about the people I missed, I was going to live among them once again and write books about a culture that like Andy's Mayberry, was bigger than the sum of its parts; a place people ought to remember.

I had accomplished as much as I could do with The Dillards during the 'growing-up' period we are all allowed before we have to settle into our life's work. I had been there for a lot of events that I would have missed back home, like watching the Beatles give kids a new way to look at pop music, and while they were at it, give the Dillards a new way to look at our own. I would have missed going on tour with the Byrds and later with Elton John, getting to meet people like Bob Dylan, Ricky Nelson, Tex Ritter, and Judy Garland, and see what *that* level of being famous was about.

I had also gotten to work with people who were just developing their crafts, like Roger Miller, Bob Denver, Steve Martin, Pat Paulsen, and Linda Ronstadt. I'd been there to watch the Smothers Brothers become TV stars and I got to meet Moms Mabley, Ernie Ford, Roy Acuff, and Gene Autry before they died. I got to play music for the cast of *Gunsmoke* on a set that smelled of horse manure and real beer from the taps of the Long Branch Saloon. I got to ride in Andy Griffith's old Ford station wagon, full of cigarette wrappers and bottle caps, and I got to dress for the Disneyland stage in Captain Nemo's original submarine used for the movie. I got to hold Joan Baez's hand at a concert while 50 of us sang a song about America, and I got to walk on the set of *Gone With The Wind*, that began where Floyd the barber's lawn left off in the fictional town of Mayberry at the edge of MGM's lot. I had gotten to experience, in other words, almost every form of fantasy that I would need. Now it was time to go back home and see whatever reality had become by this time.

I was ready for it.

Douglas "Darling" Dillard

Ozark Words

E·F·G

Encumbrance *A burden* —
"*They hated to take on the encumbrance of a mortgage.*"

Endeavor *(used as an adjective)* —
"*He'll do his endeavor best.*"

Enduring *During the time of* —
"*Enduring of World's War II we couldn't hardly get no tires.*"

Et *Ate* —
"*Now don't go to any trouble we already done 'et.*"

Faculty *(as a verb) Understand machinery* —
"*I can't faculty one of these calculators that the kids uses.*"

Fit *Fought* —
"*Those people fit and shot and thowed hatchets.*"

Foreanent *(pronounced Fernent or Forenenst) Catty-corner* —
"*The blacksmith shop used to set right fernent the courthouse.*"

Fraction *An altercation, a fight* —
"*My kids are always gettin' in a fraction with the neighbor kids.*"

Froward *Obstinate, contrary* —
"*That gal is so froward if you were to drown her she'd flow up stream.*"

Genteel *High class* —
"*We always had a truck, we didn't have no genteel car.*"

Gee-haw *Conflicting directions -or- indications* —
"*The doctor give her some medicine that gee-hawed what she was already takin' and knocked her out.*"

Chapter Five
Home Again

I came home to find the Ozarks had changed, but not all that much, sort of the way the woods change subtly when you turn your back a minute and turn around to see a deer standing where he hadn't been last time you looked. Salem, Missouri, home of the

Dillards, was very much as we had left it twelve years ago, with only small physical changes it took a while to see.

I didn't intend to live in town so that level of change didn't matter. Towns change but people usually don't. However, the lead mines had opened since I left, drawing a lot of miners in from other places like Michigan and Minnesota. These folks had brought their own kind of language, and ways of pronouncing words. Along with that, they had brought the mining culture, a way of looking at life as sort of a business opportunity, like following the wheat harvest. It was a curious mix to add to the Ozark culture which saw life more as something you were supposed to enjoy as you went along.

There was now a Wal-Mart store where a pasture had been, a Casey's General Store and gas station where a house once stood. The willow bridge, one of Salem's landmarks, was gone. The willows had died from highway chemicals put on the old bridge in winter and no one had cared enough to replace them. Some of the buildings around the square had different names on them and several houses had gone to make parking lots. There was even an all night convenience store out on the highway that sold liquor, which was pretty amazing in an area that had 72 churches and had always gone to bed at 10:00 p.m.

The place, otherwise, looked pretty much the same. KSMO had moved to bigger quarters and was now under new ownership. The old building at the foot of the Hickory Street hollow where I had once done my outrageous radio show was now a pawnshop. The high school up by Bonebrake spring was now a middle school and a huge new high school had been erected at the edge of town.

These were all changes I had expected, knowing that no part of the world stands still in the age of TV and computers.

The real, meaningful changes were more subtle, but it didn't take me long to see what they were.

The one room schools were long gone of course, but more important so were the little communities that surrounded them like Waterfork, Metham, Gill, Warfel, and Stone Hill. The little grocery store/gas station places where the school bus stopped and rural folks could pick up their mail—places that had once served as information centers for these little school communities—were having a hard time; their business going to the super markets and convenience places in town. Wholesalers, caught up in the 'big picture' of mass sales had no time to make deliveries to these little out of the way places and the crossroad stores were slowing dying.

My old friend Jimmy Butler, whose little country grocery store had served generations of neighbors stopping by to visit and pick up a sack of cracked corn or 50 pounds of dog feed, now had to drive to town himself and load these things up. The wholesaler who had brought his gasoline for 35 years was now finding fault with his small storage tank that they said didn't

come up to EPA standards. The wholesale house that had been happy to supply the odds and ends of country living that Jimmy sold to his customers had found that stores like Jimmy's weren't practical in the big picture of economic feasibility and made it impossible for Jimmy to compete unless he was willing to also take the place of the middle man, buying what he needed to sell in town.

If Jimmy had been a young man, he could have probably made the transition, but Jimmy was in his seventies and could no longer shoulder all the weight of supplies like corn and feed, much less be gone from his little store long enough to shop for all of his customers. His wife became ill and could no longer go out to pump gas and wait on customers while Jimmy made the trip to Salem. Jim's children, like a thousand other Ozark kids of that time, had moved to the city to make lives for themselves and had no interest in rural store keeping like in the old days, when children took over their father's businesses. Jimmy, who had high aspirations for his children wouldn't have wanted it otherwise, but it left him no options.

The writing was on the wall and as a collector of small stories and Ozark ways of telling them, I could see that the lines of communication were coming down. The small places where stories were told in wintertime around a Cannonball or Charter Oak stove—stores like Jimmy Butler's—were disappearing at an alarming rate, victims of the times. Back in the old days I had gathered most of my old time speech and ways of telling stories around these places, from the barber shop or the harness shop downtown or from visiting at people's houses.

That last was, I guess, more important than all the other things when it came to people communicating and passing stories along to the next generation. Ozark people had loved visiting more than any people I had ever lived among, and when I first came down I thought it was almost an obsession with them. Even before I had left, I'd seen that TV had made a big difference in the socializing that people did. Folks who had for years loaded up the family and gone over to the neighbors for a visit, didn't do it as often. Nobody wanted to miss *Gunsmoke* or *I Love Lucy*, *The Real McCoys*, or *The Andy*

Griffith Show. People had begun to stay home, not just to eat supper in front of the amazing tube but to remain there until bedtime.

By 1974, daily or even weekly visits seemed to be a thing of the past, supplanted by an overall 'busyness' that consumed everyone's time.

The other major thing I wondered about was what had happened to Saturday, which by some strange alchemy, was gone. Vanished from the weekend was the day rural people came to town. No longer did they mob Salem's square on "Trading Day" to talk and visit, and pay their bills, and shop for everything they'd need the following week.

A lot of things were responsible for taking Saturday away; better roads to town, newer cars, new stores, new income from industry, and working hours that had become 'shifts,' so that everyone had a different day off. When you added to that a brand new concept about buying on credit, and even using credit cards, you had a way of life that turned the old customs around in twelve years.

So I had to change my ways too. Instead of going to the Salem square to renew old acquaintances, I went to Wal-Mart, or to the MFA [Midwest Farmer's Association] loading dock that had also moved to the edge of town, along with a bank, a couple of used car lots, and a new grocery chain store. It seemed very strange to see a town lose its center and I had to refocus to the new ways. Instead of going to a neighbor's house where the

TV was always on and the art of conversation had atrophied, I went fox hunting and coon hunting a lot now, knowing that these night hunters were perhaps the last and best of the storytellers, telling their tales secure in the confiding nature of a flickering fire, and "a little horn" of something from a bottle. The passing along of stories and Ozark ways to the next generation was intact here at least. through the hunters.

To tell you the truth, sometimes I wondered just what it was that I thought I was doing, coming back to the Ozarks to collect the past like it was worth something to people who I now suspected had been 200 years trying to escape it. If it was now everyone's wish to build a ranch house, own a boat and a 4X4 to pull it, see their children become lawyers and bankers and responsible money makers, wasn't it just a little silly for me to remember a time when people hadn't taken their children to the dentist until they could pay cash for the work because they didn't want "the encumbrance of the debt"?

No sooner would I get glum about those things and find myself forming an attitude when somebody would tell me a story and the old ways of relating things would be back, shiny as ever.

I was at the local sports shop one day, trying to find out what had become of somebody I knew when I ran into my friend Archie, who began telling me what had happened to Tarzan Golden. He knew I'd be interested in Tarzan—whose mother had named him after the

Johhny Weismuller version—because I always kept up with everything the man did back in the old times.

Our Tarzan, like the real one, had been a free spirit who lived at best on the cusp of society, and who in the old days was in jail more than Otis, Mayberry's town drunk. I best remembered Tarzan for dancing with somebody's wife at the Lone Star beer joint and getting too familiar with her. That was a good story of itself, because Tarzan, having been knocked down by the husband and addled, woke up to use his survival instinct, hitting the first person he saw, who happened in this case to be a lady woodcutter in bib overalls who had bent over to see if he was dead. She was a bad choice for Tarzan, as it turned out, fetching him a left jab with one of her massive arms that slid him under a booth, as the teller put it, "till he had to be chopped out of there like a coon."

The current story was that Tarzan had mellowed since I'd been gone, and had taken up with a widow woman named Belle. The two of them lived in a little house in the woods north of town. Belle, who was quite a bit older, had a small pension that the two helped out by walking the highway and picking up soda bottles. It was kind of touching, Archie said, to see them holding

84

hands with Tarzan being the gentleman and carrying the tow sack full of "road plunder."

*O*ne day Tarzan showed up by himself at Archie's little gas and grocery on the Rolla highway and sat down on the pop cooler to "squander an opinion" with Archie. "Tarzan never was in much hurry about anything," Archie said, "and he was set in to gab. Bought him a pack of Luckies and a sody and we talked about what Floyd's was payin' for cord wood at the charcoal plant, and was the Cardinals going to win against Cincinnati, and sich as that.

Ever so often I'd have to go out and pump gas or wait on somebody, but he kept on sittin' there, just as talkative and brash as a jay bird for maybe an hour. And finally I just happen to think he'd hardly ever come by hisself, so I asked after Belle, I says, 'How's Belle Zory doing these days?'

"And old Tarzan, he jumped up and snapped his fingers and says, 'Now dammit, I been studyin' what it was I come by fer! Archie, have you got a rope or maybe a ladder I could borry fer a while? Me and Belle was hunting bottles around that old sink hole off of Double F highway and she fell in!' "

The countryside might have changed a little since I'd been gone and people might shop at Wal-Mart for all the things they would have bought at stores on the square years ago, but basically Ozarkians were still the keepers of a sense of humor that never changed. If they no longer swapped stories on the courthouse benches or under the awnings of hospitable merchants, they still held onto them and passed them on when they had a chance.

The way I'd hear things varied from day to day. One time I stopped by Doctor Roy Mitchell's office to have him look me over for something and lucked onto one of those classic Ozark ways of seeing people.

Doctor Roy didn't look any more like an MD than I look like a bank teller. He had a calm, unhurried way about him and dressed as plainly as he talked. When somebody would ask him his name, he'd say, "Roy Mitchell," forgetting to add on the Doctor part unless you asked, so most of us forgot too. His patients, however, called him Dr. Roy and thought he was the only doctor they'd ever need. Since I had left, a lot of foreign doctors had come to town and most of them had names Ozark people couldn't even pronounce, so Dr. Roy was trusted and looked up to. Still, seeing Roy on the street, getting out of a car no better than yours and wearing one of his checkered shirts, you'd think he owned a feed store. I couldn't help comment on this.

"Roy," I told him, "if a person was hunting doctors he'd never bust a cap on you." [never fire a shot at him]

"I know it," said Dr. Roy. "The other day somebody told me I looked like I ran a canoe rental. I just never could look like a doctor to people."

Then he told me this story. . . .

"I had to have a back operation a couple of years ago and while I was getting over that, I decided to take a weekend off and go turkey hunting down in Alabama. It was still winter up here and they have a whole different season down there. I needed to get up and do something so I called up a friend of mine who knew a guide down there. He called the guide and told him to pick me up at the airport and show me where to hunt and all that. So I got on the plane in St. Louis and when we got to Tuscaloosa another turkey hunter got off with me and it turned out we were meeting the same guide.

"Well, we didn't have time to get acquainted because this other guy was in first class, but I saw he'd bought his hunting stuff from Abercombie and Fitch or one of those places and had his shotgun in a leather case. It was a Parker shotgun and I bet that case cost more than my old pump gun, and when the guide picked us up he made over that man like he

was maybe a movie star and a crippled one at that. The guide wouldn't let him open a door or lift a suitcase. I got to wondering who this guy was, if maybe I should know him from TV or someplace. You know, somebody famous I could tell Velma I'd met.

"Next morning the guide took us out in the woods and I noticed he held down the fence wire for this man to cross and even carried his gun for him. He had a little camp stool for him. That guide pretty much left me to get by on my own."

Roy laughed about that because he was a regular Ozarker and used to taking care of himself. But you could tell that he was tickled to see a grown man coddled that way.

"Well," he went on, "we both killed turkeys during that morning, and I'll be damned if that guide didn't carry that other guy's turkey and his gun both, and insisted on holding the fences for him again, while I just kind of fended for myself.

"I finally got that guide aside and told him, 'I've got to ask you who this man is that I've been huntin' with. I know he must be famous and I want to be able to tell my wife I met him.'

"And the guide told me, 'Why that man is a doctor that a friend of mine sent down from some little town in Missouri, said he had just had an operation and didn't want him to exert himself. Said, 'Now you treat him like royalty,' and I did. You could sure tell he was a doctor, couldn't you, way he was fitted out?' "

"My God, Roy," I laughed, what did you say?"

"Aw, what the heck," said Doctor Roy, "no sense embarrassing him. I just said, 'Yeah, you can always tell a doctor every time!' "

A few stories like that made up for a lot of what was missing around the square in Salem.

In order to get settled-in to the Ozarks again I moved to a little place down on the Black River in Reynolds County and stayed there until I could build myself a house in the woods. Using my own money and what my mother had left me when she died, I built a log house on 80 acres of land in the middle of the Mark Twain National forest. It turned out that this was the best thing I could have done as far as recollecting what the Ozarks was about. The people who came to help me put that house up came from all spectrums of Ozark life. After we'd worked all day we'd sit around and I'd provide the day's refreshments in the form of a case of beer. Since everybody "brought their music," as we used to say, knowing I liked it, we'd play music and listen to each other's stories until they'd go home to supper.

Once my main log man told a story he'd heard about a Shannon County farmer saying his prayers. . . .

"This old boy says, 'Lord I ain't done too bad so fer today. I haven't blackguarded or passed on no rumors and I ain't been greedy or jealous-hearted and I haven't taken your name in vain one single time. For this I'm purely thankful Lord.'

"Then says, 'But now Lord, I'm gonna get up out of this here bed directly. . . and I may need some help with these things.' "

The joke didn't get beyond, "get up out of this here bed," until every one of us were laughing. It was such an Ozark joke, with that self-spoofing quality, that it cracked us all up.

An even better one was told by an old fox hunter who remembered me from radio days. He was a grizzled old man of 80-some, who when Howe Teague introduced me said, "Why I've knowed Mitch Jayne all my life." I remember I was tickled, being 40 at the time.

"Well, they tell this on old Clyde Beeman," he began, "and claimed it happened over at Butler's store several years back. Old Clyde, you know, he wasn't no smarter than he needs to be and could hardly read at all; jist sort of partialed [parceled] out words with his finger, one at a time, with them big bushy eyebrows all knotted in the middle. And one day there was a letter come for him in care of Jimmy Butler. Jimmy said Clyde tuck it over by the winder-light and was readin' it to hisself one word at a time and directly he says. . . .

" 'Jimmy, what does a polar bear have to do?'

"And Jimmy, that tuck him unawares, you know, and he says, 'Have to do? Well, I don't reckon he'd <u>have</u> to do anything, big as those lads are.'

"And 'ol Clyde studied about that and he says, 'Well what <u>do</u> they do then?'

"And Jimmy says, 'Well, far's I know they just sit around on the ice up there and eat fish or something.'

" 'Well then to hell with it!' Says Clyde. 'I'm a way too old fer such foolishness as that.'

"And Jimmy says, 'What on earth are you talking about Clyde, too old to do what?'

"And Clyde he says, 'Well I got this here letter from some of my connection up in Michigan. They claim my uncle Bill has died off up there and they want me to come up there and be a polar bear at his funeral.' "

Obviously all the stories were still there, all I had to do was hang out in the right places. The building of the log house was one of these, because I had hired rural neighbors with experience in carpentry, working with rock, concrete foundation work, or just putting up a log structure.

Whatever else they were, most of them were Ozark folks and the tales proliferated every time work stopped for a break. The one exception to my local help was Baxter, a man from Tennessee, but if anything, he was more of a hillbilly than any of us. He told of staying with his Grandma one time down in the Cumberland Mountains, a visit, which thinking back on it, was probably caused by some run-in with the law. He told this privately to me as we were stripping bark from logs.

His Granny, who was in her nineties, he told me, had been making a living at moonshine-making for most of her life but wanted to modernize her operation.

"Baxter," the old lady had asked him, "I'm of a great notion to try raising this marijewanny they talk about. I'm gittin' too old to be raisin' a big corn crop and wrasslin' mash barrels. Besides sugar's gettin too dear."

Baxter was startled.

"Granny," he said, "raisin' that stuff is illegal and the law can handle you for that!"

Baxter said his Granny looked at him like he was a dime short of a dollar. "Jist what do you think makin' whiskey is, which is how I've got by fer the past seventy years?"

Baxter told us the rest of the story while skinning the bark off a big pine log with a drawknife.

"Well," he said, "I got her a start of plants from a friend of mine and helped her set them out on the government." [State forestry land] "You cain't plant them on your own place or if they ketch you, they can take your farm and the clothes off your back. We'd water them at night with a five gallon bucket out of a pond and I'd he'p her to hoe weeds and put fertilize on 'em. I'd carry a little one-shot .22 with shorts to kill rabbits off them and haul water buckets for her."

I was trying to picture this little dusk to dawn farming operation ram-rodded by a 97 year old would-be drug grower and this big jovial man working next to me. I figured the story was already as funny as it could get, but I was wrong about that.

"Well, we were out there one morning early, hoeing those plants, about ten of them scattered around that old pond and Granny—she had ears like a bobcat, you know, could hear a twig snap—she looked up and tuck out her pipe and says, 'What's that?' And I looked around and God A'mighty the biggest damn helicopter I ever seen riz up from behind one of those mountains and here it come! It was one of those big wartime things with a propeller at each end and 50 caliber guns hangin' out the winders, and I knew we were screwed. And Granny, she stood there studyin' that damn thing and says, 'Baxter, shoot that thing down fer me,' jist calm as could be.

"And I says, 'Granny I cain't shoot that thing down. I've not got but shorts in this .22.' And she says, 'Well you'd best take off a-runnin then.' And I says, 'Granny, I might could get away, but you can't run and I don't want to leave you.' And she says, 'Begone whilst you have the chaince of it and don't worry about me. What are they gonna do with me? Put me in jail fer life? Hell I'm ninety-seven year old! You get along now!'"

"So what happened?" I asked. Baxter acted like the story was over.

"Well, so I made a run for it in that old church bus I'd bought, drove up here to Missouri and went to work for you." He said.

I pictured Baxter making a run for it through the Tennessee Mountains in that decrepit old bus that had a top speed of maybe forty and was the last getaway car I'd have chosen.

"Whatever happened to your Grandma?" I asked him.

"Oh she came out all right," he said, "that helicopter was a National Guard outfit out on maneuvers and wasn't after us at all."

"Did you ever go back there?" I asked him.

"Oh hell no!" Said Baxter. "That big old monstrosity of a helicopter din't turn a hair on Granny, but it scared the pee-hockey-wadding out of me. It's a way too far and snakey for me to make that trip again. And besides, I'm gettin' too old for that kind of farmin'."

We began the log house in the spring of 1975 and spent our time around an open fire after the day's work. By fall we'd gather by the huge fireplace we'd built and the stories got longer and better. There is something about a fireplace that brings out ancient ways in people, whether there is a fire in it or not. This was proven to me one evening when one of the neighbor ladies came to pick up her husband, and without thinking about it, backed up to the big stone hearth and hoisted her skirt out of habit even though it was still summer and we'd never lit a fire in it. She laughed as much as we did.

Now that we had a roof over our heads, we could quit when a thunderstorm came booming through the woods and go inside to wait it out. By this time word of my coming home to build a log house had gotten around and we would catch a lot of company every day. They were mostly old-timers who had stopped by to see if we were doing it right, or as one man said, "jist fer the novelty of watchin' them big burly logs go up."

It was on one of those rained-in days that I heard the story about the two hound men who had gotten their heads together to give old Bill Whirtle a skinning. Old

"Cooner" Bill was one of those hound traders who was as full of guile as any horse or mule trader and though usually he wouldn't flat-out lie, he was "bad to leave out the truth," as one man put it. If you wanted a turkey-mouthed fox hound or a tree dog that ran silently on the track he'd get you one with those qualities, but that was as far as his guarantee went. If the hound turned out to be a cull, or blind in one eye, a cutting dog that left the trail to second guess the fox, or spent his time fighting others in a pack, or turned out to be deaf as a snake, that was your problem. Everybody knew that if you bought a dog from "Cooner" Bill Whirtle, he'd cheat you royally "just to see if he could," as a friend told me once. In the Ozarks this kind of trading is frowned upon but accepted as part of the game when it comes to horses or hounds—a test of your own skill with animals.

I had bought a redbone hound from Bill once and old Bill had seen me coming. I bought that dog on looks alone for $500, only to find out that it was the all around stupidest animal I had ever owned and I've owned chickens. You could no more cast it on a scent than you could a plaster collie and all it was interested in treeing were my tame turkeys. The dog would neither go nor come at anybody's bidding, ran rabbits and other trash, and was dumber than a fishing worm. I used it as a yard dog—since it would bark at everyone, including the family—and finally gave it away, being too ashamed to sell it to anybody.

You can imagine how pleased I was then to hear this story told by Jim, one of my coon hunting pals, who had stopped by. This was 15 years after my skinning at the hand of "Cooner."

"Did I ever tell you about the fellers that took old Cooner Whirtle's plow through the gravels?" Jim asked. I said I hadn't but would be proud to.

"It was Jack and Harley DeWitt done it," he said, "after Cooner commenced in dealin' with all manner of dogs, not only hounds. Hell, he was tradin' whatever kind of dog you could come up with, border collies, or bull dogs, or blue heelers, didn't matter what breed. Anyway, Jack and Harley knew an 'ol buddy up in St. Louis had a pet shop and they called him up, said, 'could you come up with a one-of-a-kind dog fer us?'

"Turned out that feller had one, said it was a mutant miniature poodle, all black with kind of blue-green eyes. Said it was the onlys one he had ever seen. Well, Jack and Harley says, 'Hang onto that dog. We're playin' a trick on a feller and we're gonna send him up there to buy it. What would you have to have fer it?' Feller told 'em $300 and they says 'Don't worry, he'll pay it.'

"Well then, they got a feller from the mines they deer hunt with to come in on it, got him to call Bill and say he's heard Bill can get any kind of dog and he's desperate, let on that he's rich, you know, told Bill his wife had seen a dog on a trip they made to Beverly Hills, California, belonged to a movie star and she had to have one like it. Said it was a black miniature poodle with blue-green eyes, only he had another word for it, 'torkiss' or something.

"Turquoise?" I offered.

"Yeah, that was it. Said, 'I'll pay a $1,000 if you can get one before her birthday this week.'

"Well, 'ol Bill didn't know a thing about poodles but for a thousand dollars he figured to learn and he set in to call every dog raiser he knew and then every pet store that handled poodles up in St. Louis. Nobody had ever heard of sich a dog. But he finally come up with the right store. Feller told him, 'I've got a dog fits that description.' So Bill, he made a trip up there and bought the dog fer $300.

"When he got back he called the number the man had give him and said he'd found his dog, and the man was tickled to death. When he got to Bill's he laid out a $1,000 like it was nothin', and was just overflowin' with gratitude.

"Course 'ol Bill was feeling pretty good. He'd run up a sizable phone bill, and the trip had cost him some but he'd still sold a $300 dog for $1,000 with no investment in feed or shots, or overhead. He told down at the barbershop, says 'Hell boys, I've sold hounds fer more, but not that kind of profit.' Says, 'I may just go in the poodle business, sell rich people dogs.'

By this time all of us gathered around the big stone fireplace were hanging on this story like pins on a clothesline. I could tell that one or two had heard it before because of the way they nodded and smiled at the floor, but it was so good that like most Ozarkers they wanted to hear it again.

"Well, sir," continued Jim, "the very next week that feller that bought the poodle was back pretty near in tears. Says, 'My wife loved that dog more'n any living thing and I backed over it in the driveway this morning. She don't know it yet and if you can find me another one just like it before she gits home from her sister's tomorrow, I'll give $2,000 for it.'

"Bill he just kind of shuck his head and says, 'Feller I got it from says they ain't another like it.' But this feller won't take no fer a answer, says 'Hell, I'll give you $3,000! Money ain't nothing compared to the hell I'm gonna go through when she finds out I run over her dog.' So Bill says he'll see what he can do. After the feller's gone he calls up the pet store where he bought it to see if maybe there was another one in the same litter but the pet store man says all those pups was sold off and are spread out over no telling how far. He says he'll make a call or two and see what he can do.

"So that afternoon Bill he was hangin' in by the phone pretty tight, you know with $3,000 at stake, and along about supper time a man calls and says 'I've got a dog sounds like what you're lookin' for, I guess the litter mate, but I'd have to have $2,000 dollars for him on account of these dogs is rare and valuable,' and so on.

"Well, Bill gits to studyin' and thinks, 'well hell, that's more'n I made on the first one anyways.' So he made a trip up to Steelville, which is where the feller agreed to meet him, and paid cash for the dog, which was a spittin' image of the one he'd sold before."

I was beginning to see the light now, and one of the other listeners who had heard the story couldn't stand it and broke out laughing.

"Hell it ought to've," he gasped, "hit was the same damn dog! That old cheat bought the same dog twice!"

"And when he went to call his run-over-poodle-buyer," continued Jim grinning, "there wasn't nobody there by that name because it was a pay phone in Viburnum. 'Ol Cooner had to hold onto that dog and it 'bout killed him to look at it. He'd spent $2,000 to make less'n $700 and they wasn't nobody gonna buy the thing. He raised hell and stuck a chunk under the corner but he couldn't get no satisfaction out of nobody."

When we'd all gotten our laugh out over Bill Whirtle and his comeuppance, I asked Jim if Bill ever found out who played this incredible Ozark con game on him.

Jim said, "Well of course he knows Jack and Harley DeWitt are at the bottom of it and cain't prove a thing."

"How does he know that?" I asked.

"Well, shucks," he told me, "reason he knows, is ever time they see him they roll down the truck winder and call out 'Hey Cooner, how's the poodle business?' "

Stories like that were an ample reward for moving back to Missouri's Ozarks. Day by day the log house went up and I met more people who wanted to have a part of building it. In addition to that they had stories of their own to tell in the relaxing time after work. That happy-hour scene I had created was, in a way, the most productive time of the day for me because I was making notes on stories that would keep me busy the rest of my life.

The big house rose up out of the woods like a tree growing. The roof was composed of 30,000 shingles hand-frowed out of red oak in the old time way. The logs were hand-chinked with a plaster mix we got from a 100 old recipe and the windows bought from reclamation places from all over Missouri that specialized in old things from old houses. We made a spiral staircase from a log as big as a wagon wheel and I carved a horned owl at the top of it. A Salem blacksmith named Cecil made the step supports and the banister railing, and my old time woodworker Charley—who also built the fireplace—set in stair steps of split white oak logs. There was a touch of everyone in that house, all those people who had devoted time to its making and left their signature.

We finished the outer part of the house in October and my wife and I moved in to finish the details of the interior through the winter months. A farmer friend gave us an old cultivator wheel to set into the second kitchen chimney, from which we hung cooking pots and pans, and we hooked up one of those old combination gas/wood cook stoves to that flue. People had brought us river rock of different kinds to build into the fireplace and to lay in the kitchen floor. Later on I would be able to look at each rock and remember who had brought it.

An old Shannon County artisan, Alvy Bunch, made all the dining room chairs to go with an old table from my wife's family, which had extension leaves enough to feed a dozen harvest hands. Every beam and oak pillar of that house had a history, as easily recalled as the person who helped to set it; ten of us groaning and straining under the load of lifting a beam to its place in that house I had designed when I was 20. It is always remarkable and wonderful when dreams come true, and this house had been my dream for as long as I could remember.

When I look back on that time —and like all people my age I always do— I remember that house as the place where all the stories came together and the reason for saving them became clear in my mind. I decided, while living there, if old things and old ways are meant to be discarded—which I don't doubt for a minute—the least we can do is remember what we put behind us and record its passing; that way we'll always be able to compare new values to the old ones, and that, I suppose is the main reason I put this book together.

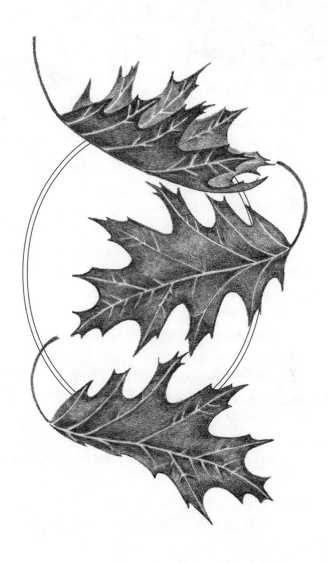

H·I·J·K Ozark Words

Hearn *or* **Heerd** Heard —
"*That's not what I been hearn, I heerd
differn't to that.*"

His'n, Her'n His and Hers as objects —
"*He taken what wasn't his'n and will have to do a turn in
jail fer that.*"

Ill Bad tempered —
"*Ever since his woman took off on him he's been ill as a snake.*"

In a manner Haphazard -or- token accomplishment —
"*Dinner is in a manner done, come when yer ready.*"

In a pile All at once —
"*Them barn cats took sick and died in a pile.*"

Infare A party or dinner given by the groom's parents
for the newly weds —
"*That marriage didn't hardly make it through the infare.*"

Infi-dell, infidel A non Christian —
"*Daddy ain't no infi-dell, he jist cain't abide churches.*"

Jilikins Wild or unsettled land —
"*That man lives so far back in the jilikins you cain't get no
regular car back to his house.*"

Jyste(s) Joist, a house timber (timbers) —
"*Them jystes were stout enough to hang a deer from.*"

Knowance Knowledge —
"*They claim she's a witch but we didn't have no knowance
of that.*"

Chapter Six

The War Between The States

Being home again, I could now take the time to figure out just what it was that made Americans laugh, so that I could work some of it into a book and make myself a living. I knew that almost all people from other countries claimed that their sense of humor was unique, but having traveled a little, I had something to compare not just Ozarkian, but American humor to. I had heard English comics make fun of Ireland, black comics make fun of white people, Jewish comics make fun of Germans, Australians make fun of England, and Italians make fun of Sicilians. I had also heard all of these people make unmerciful fun of themselves. It wasn't a quantum leap to extend what I had learned into understanding that only countries who have established a sort of national character in some way feel comfortable enough to make fun of their own people.

This was the process by which San Franciscans could make fun of LA or Missourians could make fun of Arkansas. In America we substitute areas for countries, and make jokes at each other's expense on the basis of geography rather than nationality.

What I discovered back then and am still learning about, is that Americans are such a mixture of every other culture that we get the best of it all when it comes to finding things to make fun of. We are, without doubt, the most amazing eclectic mix of colors, attitudes, customs, religions, ethnic backgrounds, politics, and prejudices under the sun, and none of us take any of them seriously enough to split the country over.

What we like to do is pick a place and give it a theme:

Q. What's the difference between Branson, Missouri, and Jurassic Park?

A. One's a theme park full of dinosaurs, the other's a movie

Q. What's the difference between North and South Dakota?

A. South Dakota Swedes say, "Aw, Jeeze you-all."

Q. Why is an Arkansas divorce like a tornado?

A. In either one, somebody's bound to lose a trailer

Missourians have always made fun of our bordering states, which are right next door and handy to us. Being in the middle of things, both geographically and economically, we are in a great position to make fun of our neighbors without anyone taking us seriously. Look where Missouri is on a map.

To the north is Iowa, a land so bland and featureless, as one Ozarkian put it that "If it wasn't for the tall corn, those people would have to look at each other's yard lights all night."

Iowa is also considered to be middle class and boring, with no imagination. "The biggest decision an Iowa cook has to make," a comedian friend from Sioux City once told me, "is whether you should serve red or white Jell-O with your tuna casserole. Iowa food just lays there, kind of like an Iowa funeral; nobody expects it to be exciting."

Kansas, to the west, is also great fodder for humorists. "Kansas," a comedian I know told his audience, "is so flat that a newspaper could blow all the way across the state without touching anyone who could read it." A Bluegrass musician I know was horrified at the pool table levelness of Kansas and described it as, "flatter'n piss on a plate." There is an old time joke about Alf Landon, running for president against Roosevelt. It was said that he couldn't campaign because traveling in any other state made him seasick. Another gag had Lizzie Borden asking Saint Peter why she had been sentenced to Kansas. Saint Peter says, "Because it's the only place hotter than hell and nobody owns an ax."

Oklahoma is even better joke material, being famous for both bailout farmers during dust bowl times and the most outrageous weather of any Midwestern state. "I knew a man one time, inherited a farm down to Ardmore, Oklahoma. He said the problem was that he'd have to go to Texas to visit his dirt."

Another story has an Oklahoma moonshiner and his son lying in a creek bottom watching a tornado carry off their still.
The son says, "Pa, what are we going to do for a living now?" His daddy says, "Now that's up to God. That tornado will either come back around with the still or come back after the mash barrels. Right now, just shut up and hang on to something."

Missouri also corners on Nebraska, which the state's humorists have pretty much left alone, most of us not being familiar with it. The residents of northwest Missouri have however, enough Nebraska jokes to make up for it.

"If it don't have four legs, moo and shit on main street, a Nebraska man don't know what it is," a man from St. Joseph, Missouri, told me, "but he'll try to rope it anyway."

Another man, talking about Nebraska's low crime rate said, "Hell, they ain't got anything to steal but cows, and they live too far apart to do that! I swear, it's a shame to make those people pay death taxes, no more'n they live!"

Illinois, on the east, doesn't fare much better when it comes to Missouri humor. "Them little towns in Illinois," a friend confided to me, "are jammed in so close together they use the same drunk, the same idiot, and the same lawyer, which is usually one man."

Astounded by the black, rock-free soil of Illinois, an Ozark man seeing it for the first time said, "Lord God, that ain't farmin, that's jist droppin' seed and jumpin' back. Farmin' is where you plow at night and see what you're doin by the sparks off the sheer!" [Plowshare]

Ozarkians in general are disturbed by flat land. "It don't seem natural to me," a neighbor told me, "to live where you cain't piss off your porch without some neighbor thinks it's a-rainin'."

When I first came to the Ozarks this sense of privacy seemed a little strange, considering the sociability of all my neighbors who seemed to spend all their free time visiting with each other. I was to discover for myself, living in the log house, privacy is something you control when you live in the woods and that is the secret of it. Ozark people just like to be in control of their own lives and those old wrinkled mountains with their hidden hollows, dense woods, and roads that snake through creek bottom crossings, suit them.

As Earl Dodson, my wood cutting neighbor said about where we lived; "When you see somebody turn in your approach, you know whoever it is *come to see you and nobody else.*"

All the eccentricities and preserved ways of looking at life that Ozarkians are known for seem reason enough to me that Missourians have always saved up their best jokes for Arkansas. This is no accident, since Missouri and Arkansas share the Ozark Mountains so equally that an Arkansas joke is pretty much one on ourselves. I hadn't been back home very long until someone sent me this imaginary application in the mail, in care of Jimmy Butler's store. Of course I didn't live in Arkansas but to the sender I might as well have, living that far back in the "jilikens."

STATE OF ARKANSAS RESIDENCY APPLICATION

Name (Male) ❑Billy Bob ❑Billy____(other) Age__(if known)
Shoe size (r)__ (l)__
Name (Female) ❑ Billie Raejean❑ Billie____(other)
Occupation: ❑Cord wood ❑Scavenger ❑Unemployed ❑Poacher
         ❑Fry Cook ❑Lube Rack ❑Moonshiner ❑Other
Spouse's
Name_____Nickname_____
Relationship with spouse: ❑Sister ❑Cousin ❑Aunt/Uncle
                    ❑Brother ❑Mother/Father ❑other_____
    Number of children in household____Number that are yours____
Mother's Names_____ Father's Names_____
Education: 1 2 3 4 5 (circle highest grade completed)
Do you: ❑Own or ❑Rent your mobile home?
Total number of vehicles you own: _____
Number of vehicles that will still run: _____
Number of vehicles to be placed: in front yard____ in backyard____
Number of firearms owned: _____
(Other weapons: ball bats, knives, re-bar, etc.) _____
Where will you keep them? ❑Truck ❑On your person ❑Bedroom
                ❑Bathroom (if applicable)❑On wall in_____room
Make and Model of your truck: 1955_____
Newspapers/magazines you subscribe to:
   ❑The National Enquirer ❑Wrestling Digest ❑TV Guide ❑Hustler
   ❑Biker Etiquette ❑Taxidermist's Guide ❑other_____
Bug screen on front of your pick up says:
❑Born To Be Wild ❑ _____ and _____ ❑Get In The Truck Bitch
Favorite Country Music: ❑Rockabilly ❑Hillbilly ❑Sadabilly ❑Sweatabilly
                ❑Elvis ❑Accordion
Favorite Family Sport: ❑Dog Fights❑Wrestling ❑Bowling ❑Cock Fights
         ❑Feuding ❑Bar Fights ❑Fights With The Old Lady
Hood Ornament on your truck is:❑Bulldog ❑Cow horns ❑Sharpened
                ❑Swan with eyes that light up
Political Party: oRepublican ❑Democrat ❑Klan ❑Oral Roberts Party
         ❑ Whichever one Daddy belongs to ❑Say Whut?
Religious preference: ❑Hard-shell Baptist ❑Holy Spirit Snake Waving
    ❑____Baptist ❑Pentecostal ❑Foot washing Baptist
❑Our Lady Of The Seizures ❑Thankee Jesus Assembly ❑One you made up
Length of intended stay in Arkansas: ❑Till welfare is established
    ❑Till Welfare checks are due ❑Till Fruit Pickin' Time is over
❑Till Uncle Billy_____dies and leaves you guns, dogs and double-
wide and surviving spouse (who may also be Mom, Sister, Grandmother or
Daughter.)

   HAVE SOMEONE FILL OUT THIS FORM FOR YOU AND SIGN (X)HERE

   _____

I not only don't know who sent me this marvelous piece of stuff, I don't have any idea who made it up. It's just one of those filings for which I've always been a magnet. Since it arrived in the 1980s, I can only suppose that it has since been improved, added to, and rewritten a dozen times with local wits adding their two-bits worth. Missourians tend to do that. Humor, as I found out early on, belongs to everybody and now blessed with the immediacy of computer communication, everyone can get in on this ancient game of making fun of whoever we think is the next rung down on the ladder.

Twenty-nine years after my application for Arkansas citizenship arrived in the mail I received a wonderful list of etiquette dos and don'ts suitable for the Arkansas family and attributed to Martha Stewart. They could have attributed it to Emily Post, the arbiter of my generation's rules for polite living, or to whoever is up next as a maker of rules, because it is timeless.

"Live stock as a wedding present
is usually in poor taste."
Martha is quoted as saying.

She goes on to suggest that the Arkansas hostess. . .
"Avoid using as a table centerpiece, anything
prepared by a taxidermist."

This kind of stuff, while pretty esoteric when compared to the usual "Don't wipe that baby's nose on your sleeve, it's not sanitary! Use the dish rag"—kind of thing—still manages to convey the message that some people aren't as civilized as we are.

These are some of my favorites in this latest batch:

❖ Never clean your ears in public. Use a private place and your OWN truck keys.

❖ On a first date, the gentleman will bait his date's hook.

❖ Establish with parents the time your date is expected home. If it is 10 p.m. be sure to dump her off by then. If it's Monday, be sure she is back in time for school.

And on other occasions:

❖ Never relieve yourself from a moving vehicle while driving.

❖ Never take a beer to a job interview.

❖ It's considered tacky to take a cooler to church.

And this last observation about gentility:

❖ It's impolite to lay rubber in a funeral procession.

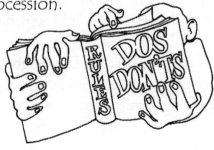

Most of these "put down" concepts I've read come under the heading of redneck jokes and aren't really applicable to the Ozarks. Ozarkians aren't rednecks at all, not having given a lot of time to remembering the War Between The States or southern attitudes. The typical Ozarkian has his own set of attitudes in which neither the North nor the South has ever figured much.

"I dis-remember which side my granddaddy was on," an old man told me one time when I asked about the War Between The States. "I figured whichever side won we knowed we'd get the moonshine contract."

What was funny to me when I was researching that war for a book was that it was the northern part of Missouri that leaned toward the Confederacy. Ozarkians to the south, not being either slave owners or large landowners, tended to stay with the Union side that had never bothered them much. The state of Missouri was so split on the political issues that it was common for both armies to recruit soldiers in the same town.

All the old mountain people wanted was to be left alone. Most of them had never seen a black person and didn't know what all the fuss was about. They couldn't take seriously the idea of seceding from a government that didn't exist for them, anymore than they were about to leave a crop in the field to go fight somebody for that government.

I learned about this best when I taught school and realized that unlike anywhere else in the South my kids had never had any family indoctrination concerning history. When I attempted to tell the sixth graders about the 'Civil War', as their history texts called it, one of my students brought me up short. "Mama says bein' civil means bein' polite." She told me, "How could folks have a polite war?" From then on I kept in mind that I was dealing with an old language that still used terms like "keep a civil tongue in your head!" I realized I couldn't take for granted things that I supposed them to know and that reminds me of a story.

I took all my students to the state capitol in Jefferson City. It was their first trip out of Dent County. I wanted them to see what a city looked like, and explain what a seat of government was. I got a friend to take us all up in his old school bus. I might as well have taken them to Oz for all of the reality they absorbed. I wanted to show them the rotunda and the great seal of Missouri in the marble floor. I wanted them to see the Missouri River and the House of Representatives and other big things, but I also wanted to show them Jesse James' pistol and a Confederate uniform and the Thomas Hart Benton murals that told our history better than I could. As it happened, I lost them before I got to the State Seal. They had gotten no farther than the old Negro janitor sweeping the floor of the rotunda and were clustered around him politely, as if he were a display. None of these children had ever seen a black person before and they viewed him much the same way a city child would look at the animatronic Abe Lincoln at Disneyland.

On the way home I confided to the bus driver that the big hit of my all day field trip had been a Negro janitor. I guess I expressed my frustration at trying to teach history to kids who didn't even know about the present yet. Ben, the driver said; "Aw hell, if I was you I wouldn't charge my mind with sich as that. When I was ten year old, I thought the President lived in St. Louis and all the weather started at Winony."

That concept made me laugh in spite of myself.

"Why would the weather start at Winona?" I asked him.

"Well hell," he said, explaining for me the way Ozark people have looked at things for 300 years, "it has to start someplace, don't it?"

I think that the best way to explain Arkansas jokes is to say that Missourians describe what they think their worst or most primitive habits are as Arkansas habits. Ducks shot on the water or quail in a bunch on the ground are referred to as "Arkansawed." A temporary repair is called "in a manner" repairing, or "Arkansawing." A particularly dumb or clumsy man is described as someone who "just rode in from Arkansas on a load of turnips."

That reminds me of my favorite Arkansas story.

*T*here was this old hillbilly bachelor feller from Booger County Missouri decided he wanted to see the ocean. He'd seen pitchers of it, you know, and heerd tell of it, but he hadn't never been anywheres near an ocean and he was curious about it.

So he hunted up one of them travel agencies and went in there and says, "I want to go on one of them sea cruises to somewheres."

Says, "Where don't matter a bit to me, I jist want to see the ocean. I want the cheapest cruise you got."

And the travel agent he says, "Surely not the cheapest," says, "you'd want a few extries on a trip like that, you're not ever a-goin' to do it agin'."

But this old hillbilly, he's got his mind set, you see. "No sir," says, "alls I want is to smell salt water, maybe see some seagulls, feel them waves a bobbin' me." says, "I want the cheapest thing you got."

"Well all right," says the travel man, "that'll be $29.95." The hillbilly commences counting out the money, and while he's dedicated to doin' that the agent reaches down under the counter and gits a big old leather maul out and pecks him right top of the head with it, and down he goes.

Well, when he wakes up there he is a floatin' in a barrel in the Gulf of Mexico. Well, directly he looks around and here is an Arkansas feller floatin' in another barrel. He can tell he's from Arkansas on account of he has scars all over his face from learning to eat with a knife and fork.

This Missouri man he wants to be sociable so he paddles over to the Arkansas man and pecks on the barrel and says, "Pardon me, but is this here the $29.95 Sea Cruise?"

And the Arkansas man says, "Why, yes it is. Welcome aboard."

And the Missouri feller says, "Well, these is kind of shabby accommodations," says, "do they serve breakfast on this here cruise?"

And the Arkansas feller says, "Well now, they didn't <u>last</u> year."

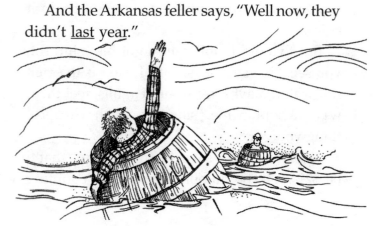

I have found out over a lot of years experience that this is what the <u>current</u> War Between The States is all about; in this case, the gentlest, funniest battle of cultures you could imagine. After all, it is about geography and not really about differences between people. I've become convinced that all of us need to believe that some segment of our society is screwed-up and the rest of us are all rational. We can make fun of the screwed-up ones, picking them out by areas, states, colors, religions, politics, strange beliefs, and so on. Basically we all need to express a sense of humor about the fix we're in.

What always seems funniest to Ozarkians are people who have decided to nit-pick details in a world full of gigantic problems of survival. The mountain people, always living from season to season, have forevermore wondered about these people who find time to become worry-specialists; like people who handle rattlesnakes for religious reasons, Jehovah's Witnesses, people against wearing hides or fur, vegetarians, astrologers, end-of-the-world prognosticators, nonsmokers who suppose that cigarettes are more toxic than the engine fumes we breathe, people who build bomb shelters, folks who think computers will solve all of our human failings, folks who think firearms cause crime, and people who watch as their children listen to music played at a louder level than blowing up stumps with dynamite.

121

Ozarkians don't preach against these attitudes they just wait them out and make up funny stories about them, usually with a hidden moral, and this is the secret, if it ever was a secret, to Ozark humor. It allows us to see how ridiculous we get when we pretend that we have some special edge on getting through life. One of the best stories I know to illustrate this is one I had a part in.

I was riding in a car one time with my friend Basil who was driving way too fast for the road we were on. I cautioned him about a farm up ahead where the house was across the road from the barn and there were always a bunch of guinea fowl out picking in the road. Basil began telling me about guineas, which he said were the smartest bird next to a wild turkey he knew about. "Now chickens will just mill around and get in their own way when a car comes by," he said, "but your guinea, he has better sense than that. Them things can dodge a bullet. You just wait and see."

Over my protests Basil didn't slack a bit and we came tearing around a little curve to find about fifty guineas dusting and scratching in the middle of the road.

"Now you watch this!" said my friend as we plowed into the flock, "I won't touch a feather."

The next thing I knew there were guineas all over the windshield, under the car and splattered all over the radiator. One flew into the open window and broke her neck on Basil's forehead. Altogether this science demonstration killed six guineas and the car looked like a chicken coop floor.

I couldn't wait to hear Basil explain his unkillable guinea theory to the owner of the flock, but there was no one home. Basil and I picked up dead guineas and put them in the truck and he stuffed five dollars in the farmer's mailbox. Back then that would cover the price of his destruction, which was a good thing because that was all he had.

I waited patiently for the good hillbilly excuse I knew was coming.

"Those couldn't have been regular guineas," said Basil finally, a mile or two down the road. I noticed he had slowed down considerably. "They must of brought them up from Arkansas."

Ozark Words

Lavishes *A pretty plenty -or- a great plenty —*
"You can stay all night we got lavishes of room."

Least *Youngest, smallest —*
"Why he's a old man, his least 'un's fifty-years old."

Lenth *Length —*
"Pa fell and measured his lenth on the ground."

Meander To *take a wavering path - wander —*
"That boy meanders around like his daddy."

Melt *The spleen, Courage —*
"He wants to tell her off bad right, but ain't got melt to do it."

Mend *To improve - to fix - to tend —*
"You help your maw and mend the fire while I'm gone."

Mind *Pay attention to —*
"Mind about runnin' out of gas on the way back."

Mirate *Exclaim over - Admire —*
"He takes a sull if you don't mirate over his good grades."

Miration *General admiration —*
"He done his best, but nobody made no great miration over it."

Misdoubt *Doubt —*
"Been so long, I misdoubt I'd know his face."

Misling *A drizzling rain or mist —*
"Hit was an all day mislin' rain that spoiled that hunt."

Mistook *Mistaken —*
"I think he's mistook in his politics, but I like him fine."

Mistress *Mrs. —*
"We'd like to do this song for Mister and Mistress Gibbs."

Mought *Might —*
"Ask him, he mought could come too."

Chapter Seven

Would You Repeat That Please?

Typical Hearing Aid:

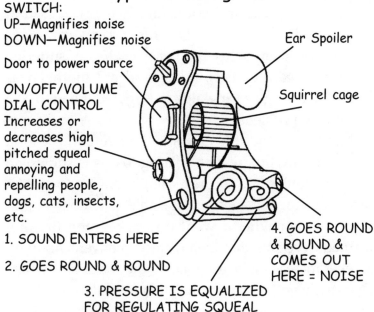

SWITCH:
UP—Magnifies noise
DOWN—Magnifies noise

Door to power source

ON/OFF/VOLUME
DIAL CONTROL
Increases or
decreases high
pitched squeal
annoying and
repelling people,
dogs, cats, insects,
etc.

1. SOUND ENTERS HERE

2. GOES ROUND & ROUND

3. PRESSURE IS EQUALIZED
FOR REGULATING SQUEAL
PITCH

Ear Spoiler

Squirrel cage

4. GOES ROUND
& ROUND &
COMES OUT
HERE = NOISE

I've thought a lot about whether I should put in a chapter about being hard of hearing since being deaf as a snake isn't all that funny, but does have a lot to do with the way things turned out for me and it might encourage other people who have hearing problems.

There is a big difference between being deaf and hard of hearing; deaf people can't hear at all, but hard of hearing people can be helped in *some way* no matter how severe the loss is. Let me put it this way; without my hearing aids, I can't hear anything at all. As a friend put it, I couldn't hear God bowling. Fortunately, I can hear because of today's hearing-aid technology.

In 1974 it was my continual hearing loss that encouraged me to leave the Dillards and make my move back to the Ozarks. My brother was already suffering from progressive hearing loss and my mother was already wearing hearing-aids so I figured it had to be a hereditary problem.

I no longer had to worry about playing music for a living but my progressive hearing loss was still going to be a problem. It got increasingly harder for me to hear someone tell a story or be able to tell one hound from another when I went on fox or coon hunts. I learned over time that the greatest inconvenience with an ever increasing hearing loss is the social one, where everybody notices it but you; and you make everybody crazy by either asking them to repeat what they said or just grin and pretend.

My hearing loss was about as gradual as hair loss and it was twice as easy to pretend that it wasn't happening. There is an old joke about that; "I'm not getting deaf, people just don't talk as loud as they used to." I would have continued to deny my own hearing loss, except I had to keep working and my work has always been listening to people.

After I came home one of the first things I did was offer my services as a substitute teacher. I wanted to see what had happened to the language and the way to find out about it was to talk to children. I contacted numerous school districts and volunteered to substitute teach on any given day at any level; first grade through high school. I was so eager to do this that I got ashamed of myself, sitting around like a buzzard waiting for a teacher to get sick.

The problem I had wasn't long in showing up. I couldn't hear the younger children, whose high vocal range was beyond my ears, and I couldn't hear the older ones when more than one spoke at a time. I was unable to decipher what was being said to me when there were other children talking in the background. I was wearing a hearing-aid by this time and lived with the frustration of now having all sound amplified at the same volume. I no longer had discretionary hearing, the ability to 'focus' on one person's voice in a room filled with many voices.

I kept trying to teach until it got ridiculous and I had to quit. I did manage to teach enough children of various ages over a year's time to discover that the Ozark speech as a daily language was extinct. I would hand out my Ozark word list to the children and ask them if they recognized any of the words and to take the list home and ask their parents too.

Sadly, the language was gone for these children. There were the occasional child's vague references to having a grandparent who spoke "mother-tongue" but it was as foreign to them as a European language. It had been 21 years since I had taught one room schools and I realized that television had allowed these children to assimilate the language that was spoken by the rest of the country. There was another influence as well, a regional one.

About the time the Dillards headed for California in the early '60s more lead mines were opening up all over the Ozarks, with the increase in mines came professional miners from other states. They moved there with their families and brought their own influences of customs, styles, and language.

After substitute teaching I took on a couple of writing jobs for a local newspaper in Salem, writing feature stories about interesting local people. This, like the substitute teaching, was all about rediscovering the Ozark culture, seeing what had happened to it and why. While I was at it, I got to hear more stories from home. One of my first features was about my old neighbor Albert Norris, whose nickname was "Goob." I will never forget sitting down to interview him in his living room and discovering that he was deafer than I was. It was humorous to see the two of us shouting at each other and misunderstanding what we did hear.

I told Goob about how I went into Jimmy Butler's store, after an absence of 12 years, and Jimmy spotting my hearing aid. Jimmy was one of the old timers who still called me "Mike" that was a nickname from radio days.

"Is that thing in your ear a hearing-aid?" he asked. I told him that it was and that I had gotten it from the Veteran's hospital.

"Does it work?" asked Jimmy. I said, "No, but it sure beats nothing and I've tried both."

"I'm gonna have to get me one." said Jimmy sadly.

I was amazed. Although Jimmy was 15 years older than I was, he had ears like an owl. I knew because I had turkey hunted with him and not only could he hear a distant gobbler better than most people, he could also tell where it was and how far away. I reminded him of that but he just shook his head.

"I guess I'm getting deaf." he said. "I embarrassed myself to death the other day, and in front of a lady, too.

"What happened?" I asked, knowing a story when it's there.

"Well, this woman pulled up by the pumps in one of those little foreign cars and I went out to fill it," he said, "and you know how little them things are. I could look down and see everything in that car and Mike you never seen such as that was, with cigarette butts and candy wrappers and I don't know what all down there, and I guess I was thinking about that when that woman pops out of the car and says, 'Pardon me, but do y'all have a rest room?' "

"And Mike, I would have sworn she said, 'Do y'all have a whisk broom?' you know, thinking about all that stuff in her car. So I says, 'Well no we don't, but if you could kindy rake it up with your hands, I've got a poke [sack] you could put it in.' "

Goob Norris thought that was as funny as I did. I told him it was the first time I'd ever heard that joke and Jimmy told it in such a mournful and serious way, it was a minute before I realized how completely I'd been had. Goob and I agreed that this was not only a testimony to Jimmy's ability to tell a story, it was also one of the things deafness will do to you if you're not careful. You start taking everything people say about deafness seriously, when it's one of the oldest forms of humor around.

I still think the funniest hearing-aid joke is the one about the guy who has a new one and is bragging about it.

"I can't believe I went so long without this thing," he tells his friends, "It's like having a new pair of ears. . . . " and he goes on about it for a while. "Hell," he says, "anymore, I can hear a mouse pissing on cotton, and I'm beginning to hear stuff people haven't even said yet," and he brags on about his new hearing-aid until finally one of the guys asks him, "What kind is it?"

And the deaf man looks at his watch and says, "Oh, about ten minutes till three."

Some of the best humor regarding hearing loss has to do with denial. Lots of Ozark men, plenty bright and observant otherwise, would deny that there was anything wrong with their hearing. One once told me. . . .

" My old woman, she says, I'm gettin' deaf. But it's not nothing in the world but that she's gettin' mush-mouthed and don't talk plain. I told her she needs to get her some teeth and quit worryin' about my y'ears."

Not only do most people not want to wear hearing aids, half the people who actually have them, never wear them because when they go to someplace like the grocery store or Wal-Mart they are hit by a cacophony of noise that blind-sides them. It is the same with watching television. I remember an old man telling me one time. . . .

"I cain't no more make out what they say on *Green Acres* than listenin' to a dog fight. They keep a laughin' and drowndin' each other out."

Hearing-aids can end up on the mantle in the Ozarks, next to false teeth that don't fit. It's one of the feelings in our part of the country that you should get by with the equipment you were born with.

One of the oldest jokes about hearing-aids was told to me by Virgil Parker, a preacher who was so old himself that he was said to have "married, carried, or buried" about everybody in Dent County. Virgil said. . . .

"There was an old man from Salem who went down to Shannon County to sit in on the funeral of a boyhood friend, and he had one of those old 'listening horns' that deaf people used to use. It was just a long curved pipe flared at

one end and you stuck the small end in your ear and turned the bell toward the sound you wanted to hear. Well, this old man tottered into church with his listening horn and one of the ushers was just a young kid, who didn't know him, and he'd never seen one of those horns. He said, 'Now I'm going to seat you down here with the rest of the departed's friends, but I warn you, one toot out of that thing and you're out of here!' "

A few years ago hearing-aids weren't much more practical than the 'hearing horn'. Nobody, it seemed, could do squat about lost hearing except hook you up to amplifiers that no more resembled hearing than a bull horn resembles speech. No one has ever thought that losing your sight was funny, but hearing loss is the sort of thing so awkward and embarrassing—sort of like being accident prone or clumsy—that people make fun of it with impunity, and of course I do too. So many of the jokes I know are based on misunderstanding, like the *polar bear* joke and the Ozarkian *whittled words*.

Most hearing-aids have plastic casings with an amplifier and a volume control that you stick in your ear.

This hard plastic doesn't really fit in the ear canal very well and there can be lots of whistling and feedback every time you smile, chew, laugh, or yawn. I was always telling people when my hearing- aids would go off like a smoke alarm that they'd work great on a dead person.

What has always aggravated me about the few companies that made hearing-aids back in those days was they all seemed to be more concerned with hiding the things rather than the fact that they were supposed to help me hear. It was as if hearing impaired folks were all so vain that we thought if no one saw our hearing-aids, no one would know we were deaf as swamp fungus. Just a few years ago I went in to have one of my routine hearing tests done by a popular hearing-aid company and the technician/franchise owner was more salesman than hearing expert. I was now going to have to wear a behind the ear hearing-aid because I was needing more power for amplification. Rather than tell me how my hearing would be improved with this added amplification he was more interested in telling me that they came in a variety of colors; red, royal blue, and "natural." This sort of made me wonder if the only advancement in the technology department was an improvement in the colors of plastic. When you think about how dumb that was you can understand why I was always able to see the humor in growing deafer every day. That was because I was almost daily reminded that loss of hearing, not being considered a life threatening situation, was treated more as a one of the funny things that happen to people, sort of like absent-mindedness or a tendency to mix meanings; as in the old story about the nurse who gave ten pills at two instead of two pills at ten and inverted her directions to "prick that man's boil."

Vance Randolph, Ozark folklorist, told a funny story in one of his books about an old hillbilly and his wife. It's rarely told except around a campfire, so I'm going to put it in here before it disappears.

*T*he wife was deaf, and after getting the men coffee she went off to herself to shell peas. The old fellow was telling Vance a story, and as he did, said, "excuse me," and  lifted one cheek off the chair and broke wind. It wasn't all that noisy said Vance, but the cat reacted like it had been a gunshot and took off in a panic, damn near broke its neck getting out the screen door. The old man laughed at Vance's surprise and explained, "My old woman is as deaf as an anvil, but ain't nothing the matter with her nose. When she smells anything like shit, she grabs the broom and lights in after that cat."

135

The kind of humor my own deafness supplied was mostly of the misunderstanding of words variety, which, because I couldn't hear consonants clearly got really hilarious.

*O*nce, when the Dillards were doing a show at Churchill Downs, a fast speaking fan visited our dressing room. He told us he had seen one of our friends the week before playing at 'The Red Foreskin.' I was appalled. After the gentleman left I told the rest of them, "I can't believe anyone we know would play at a club called 'The Red Foreskin!' " That got everybody tickled but they're used to me. "That's 'THE RED HORSE INN,' Mitch!" Douglas told me, but I still believe that guy should have talked slower.

After a while those things became so commonplace I forgot to write them down, although some of them were really funny. Usually though, they were just dumb, like the time my wife Diana told me, from a room away, that I'd left the hose running and I brought her a box of Kleenex. No matter, I'll be doing more like them as the years go by.

Hearing loss doesn't get better, but technology is trying to do more to keep up these days with the things that wear out before the rest of you does, like eyes, teeth, hair and now finally, ears. Right now, battery operated amplifiers are still the best we can do, the deafer you are, the bigger the battery. I figure the next step for me will be a car battery that I'll have to carry in a sack like I was ready to jack-light a deer.

Today my hearing-aids are the best technology has to offer. I tell people that my ears are now run by computer chips. They strengthen consonants so that I can hear words more clearly and they have soft silicone ear molds that don't whistle. I even have an auxiliary hearing device that I wear on stage when the Dillards get together for reunion concerts. If I live long enough, technology will get around to ear transplants and I won't have to wear all the equipment. Of course I'll be in a home by that time, crazier than a box of rectums, but I'll be able to hear a pin drop.

I could probably communicate by writing every-thing down. Maybe I could use sign language, but as clumsy as I am I would not only break things at the dinner table with all that hand waving, but I would probably not get words right. Instead of saying, "Thank you for the wonderful dinner," I would probably be sign-ing, "I think I have just ruptured myself," which reminds me of another joke somebody sent me.

137

A little boy was telling his dad about his friend's uncle who was deaf. "He doesn't talk at all, he just makes words with his hands."

Dad thought about that and decided to try out the kid's sense of humor.

"Wonder what he does when he wants to yell?" he said.

"He doesn't have to," said his son, "he doesn't have any kids."

*S*ince the only really funny part of being deaf is the mishearing of things, which I know for a fact is sometimes hilarious, I think I have saved the two best stories for last, one of them being about a 100 years old and the other pretty recent.

*I*n the 100 year old story, a deaf old man is looking for his cow when he meets a preacher cutting through the woods to his church. The preacher invites him to come to church and says that after the sermon he will ask his congregation to keep an eye out for the lost heifer.

The old man goes with him and sits through the sermon even though he only hears about one word out of ten. After the sermon the preacher begins talking about a young couple who will be married the following week. The bride is a local girl so he goes to some length to describe her glowingly. The old deaf guy, thinking that the preacher is at last talking about his missing cow, stands up and shouts; "And besides that, she is bobtailed and has a scarred tit from bob-wire."

*T*he more modern one is about an old friend of mine who fought hearing-aids "until the last dog was whupped," as his wife put it. The turning point came while he was out in his machine shed listening to a local radio station going full blast over the noise of machinery. When his wife brought out his lunch the news was on and the announcer had just said that Turkish forces were fighting with Kurds at the border.

"Mother," said Everett, "either I need hearing aids or them Turks is using the damnedest ammunition you ever heard of."

N·O·P· Ozark Words

Needments *Necessaries* —
"*She carried a big budget [purse] with all her needments.*"

Neer-a *Never* —
"*There was neer-a vote cast fer him in <u>this</u> town, I'll warrant.*"

Norate *To make public - Broadcast* —
"*I've heerd it norated, but it ain't in the paper.*"

Our'n *Ours* —
"*We rented that property for years but now it's our'n.*"

Plat *To braid or plait* —
"*He wore his hair platted like a Indian.*"

Plumb *Total, complete - also vertical* —
"*He gets drunk and staggers around out of plumb.*"

Plunder *Personal belongings* —
"*He gathered up his plunder and moved in with the family.*"

Poke *A sack* —
"*He brings his lunch in a poke, most days.*"

Ponder *To think out* —
"*She don't ponder nothin', just flies in an does it.*"

Posts, Nests etc. *See "Beastes"*

Preachment *A sermon - a set of rules* —
"*You kids want a preachment or a whipping?*"

Professor *A believer, one who professes religion* —
"*Them old professors is so ignorant they mess with rattlesnakes.*"

Proffer *To Offer* —
"*She proffered us coffee but I don't use it.*"

Chapter Eight

Bunker, Missouri,
And Life Among The Storytellers

Back home again with the time to do some serious writing, I didn't really know how to go about it. What I wanted to do was to capture the Ozarks for people who might never visit the place. I wanted to picture for them, the kind of people who would keep a language of their own for 200 years, simply because it said things the way they saw them.

I decided first of all, to do a book about Bunker, Missouri, a little town in Reynolds County that was the most self-sufficient community I had ever seen. It also had the most down to earth form of government, with two people who took turns being mayor. When the town's citizens thought one mayor had been in too long or he made them mad enough, they tried the other awhile. To ensure civility the city council members brought firearms to meetings and stacked them in a corner—a symbolic gesture in case of intimidation. The town had some 400 citizens who wanted no part of state or federal aid and did everything for itself, independent of outside agencies.

I didn't know if a book about a self-sufficient town would sell, but like most people who had already sold a book, much less had it made into a film as I had, I thought I could probably do no wrong. I lit into writing the book, operating on memory alone, confident that my idea would be as saleable as salt.

When I first saw Bunker, Highley's General Store was the town center and in front of the steps was a giant, permanent puddle in which a hog was wallowing. People walked around the wallow and usually spoke to the hog before they went in. Inside the store were feed, seed, groceries, hardware, tires and batteries, saddles and tack, clothing, the post office, the bank, and probably the phone company.

It was love at first sight for me and 50 years later Bunker is still my ideal town, entirely good natured, fond of its own eccentricities, and in no hurry to see progress change either the look or meaning of their lives. I picked another name for my town and changed a lot of the background, but I peopled it with citizens comprised of characters I had known for years and gave it a problem to solve: *What do you do when the government wants to change you for your own good?* In this case, covering the little town I renamed *Morning Glory* under 50 feet of water. They would do this by damming their spring branch in order to make a multi-purpose lake. A lake that could either pay them three times what their land was worth, thereby making them rich by Ozark standards, or make them all lake property resort owners.

The first person to find a place in this proposed book was a character based on Zeke Dooley, who you met several chapters back, talking about moonshine whiskey. Zeke was a prototype for all the Ozark natives who had chosen to live by their own rules. Zeke was always at his best while being interviewed. His specialty was entertaining himself at the expense of the interviewer. This is a typical Zeke interview taken from the radio shows I did in the 1950s.

The most forgivable thing about Missouri's weather, according to our Ozark expert Zeke Dooley, is that it never lasts long enough for a person to work up a serious complaint. To avoid cabin fever, I made a visit to Booger County last week to get Zeke's take on the winter of '56. I tape recorded the results:

Mitch: Zeke, how does this winter compare to others you've known?
Zeke: Well I ain't been disfurnished much out of the ordinary. This snow makes it a heap easier to drag in a deer.
Mitch: But harder to get around, I'd think, just out and about.
Zeke: Well actual, ain't much to git out and see, 'cept other folks's snow. Ain't no better'n our'n fur's I kin tell.
Mitch: You keep a good stock of groceries?

Zeke: 'Bout like a general store. The wife, she's a lot like a squirrel comes to winter vittles.

Mitch: So you stay pretty much at home?

Zeke: Till it gets so boresome we have to go some'ers fer the novelty.

Mitch: Can you always tell when it's time to get out of the house?

Zeke: When the old worman falls to studyin' me and directly says; "Ezekial, I believe you are the sorriest use fer skin of ary critter I know." It's time fer her to go to a catalogue store or either one of them beauty saloons.

Mitch: And how about you? Do you get testy at all?

Zeke: Naw, I'm natured like a old hound, jist lay by the fire. . . toss me a bisquit now and then and the only growl ye hear's my belly. It's Perletta that suffers the shut-ins.

Mitch: By the way, where is your wife?

Zeke: Why, somebody at church lent her a pitcher puzzle to put together— that's it spread out over the kitchen table yonder.

Mitch: Oh, I see it. She has it all done . . . but. . . there's a piece missing.

145

Zeke: Yep. And now she's took off in a foot of snow to track down that there piece and trade the varmint that left it out a piece-of-her-mind.
Mitch: Uh-oh!
Zeke: You could say that. A piece of Perletta's mind this time of year would burn a hole through a Jehovee's Witness. And while yer in the kitchen there, jist toss me one of them bisquits.

Zeke was the most useful character I knew. He was a composite of all the old men I had listened to around campfires and the heating stoves of country stores; a subsistence farmer, trapper, woodcutter, hound man, hunter, and moonshiner rolled into one. In the old days I could use him for political comment or comic relief, for weather prophecy or hunting advice. He worked so well for radio that I invented a wife for him, Perletta Dooley, who always expected the worst and forecast it like a Dickens character. She was modeled after a farm wife I had met, whose favorite expression on hearing that a neighbor had a close call with death was, "I guess that's the way he'll go." I think the first time I used her in a magazine was this one in *Today's Farmer*, some 30 years later. They hadn't changed a bit. . . .

Every now and then I have to make a trip back home to visit Zeke and Perletta Dooley. They live in a cabin on Blair's Creek, where the narrow road, the big woodpile, and yard full of hounds all speak of another day and time. But not as much as Zeke and his wife do. . . .

Mitch: How are you folks?

Zeke: Why we're tolerable, I reckon.

Perletta: Speak for yerself. I ain't been any account since I fell on the ice and yaunched a hinge in my back.

Zeke: Comes from trying to pack a whole deer from the smoke house.

Mitch: By herself?

Zeke: Yep. Told her she should have cut it in half, made two trips.

Perletta: I'd fergot to put ashes down and my trotters went out from under me. Slid pert-nigh to the creek on that black ice.

Zeke: I heerd it plumb to the house! 'Bout whittled my thumb off, thought a cow'd got down.

Perletta: I guess that's the way I'll go.

Mitch: I worry about you still using that old privy when there's ice on.

Zeke: Well we know that path y'see. Perletta kin skip down it glib as a quail.

147

Perletta: Yes, when it ain't froze slicker'n deer guts on a door knob I can. I've told Ezek'l they's some our age has indoor plumbing.

Zeke: Yes, and most our age don't need no plumbing, count of they're dead.

Mitch: Yeah, but Zeke, your privy is 50 yards from the house. That's a long hike in winter time.

Zeke: In winter time that's 50 yards too far, but in summer time, it's 50 yards too near. I jist know tain't going in the house.

Perletta: I wouldn't mind so much, but for the hounds using in there this bad weather.

Mitch: You let the hounds use the privy?

Zeke: Well, not in the usual way, of course. But serval of them get in there when the wind cuts. Perletta, she got 'em started on that, put a rug down.

Perletta: Well a body had to. The place draws like a flue to where it's like perchin' on a chimbley and hit's so out of plumb you cain't keep the door buttoned and. . . .

Mitch: I'm sorry I brought it up.

Imaginary character Perletta Dooley

Zeke: Dad fetch it Perletta, you run on like ary windmill. When I was a boy wormen folk didn't talk brash about sich as toilets. If a worman had to use one, she'd say; "I have to go outside."

Perletta: When you was a boy Ezek'l that was likely the only place to go. I just wish that before I die I could have a place to where I didn't have to lean out and jerk on the door like yankin' up a well bucket.

Zeke: Now Perletta, I'm a layin' off to fix that place up fer ye, come green-up time.

Perletta: Zeke'l that's what you said 53 year ago, come February.

Zeke: There! See how the time gets away when you're enjoyin' yourself?

Mitch: And I believe getting away is what I better do!

I worked on the book about Morning Glory, (which I called *The Glory Hole War*,) for nearly three years, getting my life back into its natural writing function. I always tried to work five or six hours a day, or night, at the typewriter to get some sort of discipline going. When I had written my second book, *Old Fish Hawk*, I had been forced to do all my writing between Dillard jobs; working at the book in motel rooms while we were on the road, and in my backyard when I was home. Since Fish Hawk was one of the last Osage Indians in Missouri and the story was placed in the late 1800s, working on the book was one of the strangest time warps you could imagine. Lots of times I would get home from doing a television show in Hollywood and sit down at 2 a.m. to read what I'd written 24 hours before. It was confusing, but comforting in a way, to be able to plunge myself back in time to the wooded bluffs above the White River and the Ozarks I remembered so well. That was the real discipline, forcing myself between centuries. Compared to that, writing at home again should have been a breeze.

I had a young man's confidence; after all my second book had gone into paperback and later had become a motion picture. Surely every word I wrote would be saleable.

But there was so much else to do having come home, and so many things to get caught up in. It was time to recapture all the Ozark history that had made me write *Old Fish Hawk* in the first place.

That autumn, after we had moved into the log house, I bought a coon hound or two and began to take up coon hunting again. If you have never done this, I should probably try to tell you why anyone hunts with hounds at night. It is a sport as old as man, or maybe I should say a sport as old as man's relationship with dogs. A hound does what he does best, which is to use his nose to solve a puzzle, and a human listens to him and goes to the dog to reward his dedication to that puzzle. It's a sport that neither the under-civilized, nor over-civilized would enjoy much, sort of a chess game for those of us who like to watch nature up close. I needed to get back to the basics. There is magic to a Missouri night and a mystery to traveling in strange woods following the distant sound of hounds. As the dogs unravel the raccoon's trail you begin to understand what a clever, inventive, and elusive animal like a raccoon can do with his knowledge of the countryside.

When I was a kid, I used to hunt coons all night long, following the hounds on foot over miles and miles of the flat land that is north Missouri. But now, in 1975, I wasn't a kid anymore. There isn't anything flat about the Ozarks and I was in poor shape to pull those steep hollows that coon's and hounds traveled as easily as level ground.

I took a friend's advice and bought a jumping mule, a small variety that would not only carry you all night through the mountains, but would jump fences, follow the hounds, and climb into the back of a pickup truck as obediently as any dog. Most of the coon hunters my age had bought one of these little mules and our hunts became the sort of gatherings that deer camps had always been; social clubs founded on the basis of a love for the woods by people who knew them well. Storytelling was as natural to this bunch as hound music and the many pauses, waiting for a hunt to take shape were always an opportunity for stories. I'd listen and make mental notes and when I got home (sometimes just before daylight,) I'd write the bones of the story down so I could later do a more complete job. Some of these stories I wrote later on for magazines, changing the names of the people, and altering the story to suit the market. The stories themselves usually took this form. . . .

Speaking Well of the Dead

*O*ne of the things we don't do anymore in these automated times is dig the graves of friends and neighbors ourselves. When someone dies, nowadays, the old neighborly chores are taken over by the machinery of progress and the funeral people see to everything.

But in the Ozarks of the 1950s it was still the custom to have family graveyards that usually ended up as small community burial sites. We all figured that if you had managed to neighbor with someone all those years, there was room to accommodate their company below ground too. Occasionally, we would plant people who hadn't spoken in years in the same plot and sometimes we were a little dubious about putting people who had fought every time they met, in the same chunk of ground, especially if they had been married to each other.

Each time one of the old "residenters" would die out it was expected that every neighbor would bring a shovel and his lunch pail, and join the grave digging crew. I always found it rewarding work, for if the neighbor was colorful and well liked, the stories would fly thick and funny, and always pleasant. In the Ozarks it's part of the ceremony to remember the departed with good humor. The most observed custom of our folks, whether based on superstition or simply good manners, is to never speak ill of the dead.

But I have to tell you about the time when we buried possibly the most spiteful, hateful old fellow on the creek. He had died on the hottest day of the year, and I wouldn't be surprised if he hadn't done it on purpose, leaving his wife and his neighbors to put up his hay.

I wasn't really looking forward to this grave digging, not so much because it was 80 degrees at 8:00 in the morning, as that I hadn't really liked the man and even talking about him was going to be unpleasant.

Looking around at my fellow diggers, I realized that at one time or another every one of us had been cheated, shorted, or sheared by the old wretch, and I wasn't the only one trying to think of something light-hearted to say.

For a long time we worked in silence, each person doing his best to come up with some positive story to tell about Wilber Meekins, deceased. I had never seen any of my jovial neighbors so quiet.

Discomfort grew. Now and then we all stopped and looked at each other and passed the water jug around. This man had beaten his hounds and starved his stock, and gone to law with his neighbors over his farm boundaries, claiming land he couldn't have used anyway. He had been tight beyond belief, so penurious in fact that he begrudged the food his wife ate, and the poor woman had never had a new dress in the 30 years they had been married. He had run off his only daughter, a teenager, so that he wouldn't have to pay for the girl's schooling and no one knew where she was.

The list of his transgressions was endless and his good-hearted neighbors struggled with it.

Finally, the oldest of these, my friend Herman Norris, stopped and stuck his shovel in the clay.

"Now boys," said Herman, "this won't do a-tall. Somebody has to come up with *something* tolerable to say about 'ol Wilber. This ain't custom, it ain't Christian, and it ain't fittin'."

We all stopped working and perched around the grave on tombstones, racking our brains. One man said that Wilber kept good horses, but another said, "Yes, and mistreated them so shameful it was a disgrace before God and all his boarders." Which scotched that hope.

One after another, we tried ideas and one after another these fell to the axe of truth. There was just nothing, in the spirit of kindness, that could be said about Wilber Meekins.

But finally, one of the old farmers who had been pensive and silent like the rest of us stood up and his eyes brightened. We all waited hopefully.

"Boys," he stated very seriously, "say what you want but that old bastard was the neatest man about his chewin' tobaccer I ever saw."

And with that lucky thought, custom was satisfied and we dug with a will.

Now, years later, I can still remember that one of the real dependable things about coun-

try people is that they can always make do with
what they have.

This was a story I heard around a fire, and what you
just read was the way a typical story went into print
later on, not much changed but put into the kind of
form someone could read and maybe chuckle at.
Storytelling is such an art form that *telling* it in print
was—and is—one of the hardest jobs I ever tackled. This
book, for instance, is mostly stories which I can't tell
you, but have written down for you, hoping that you
can identify with both the characters and me.

Let me give you another example of this strange way
of relating a story, this one in *Today's Farmer*, a magazine that bought everything I sent them for years. It
was a brand new discipline for me to learn, this business of telling a story in just so many column inches of
space, but I learned how to do it. I had 2500 words to
tell this story about "cutting dogs," no more, no less, or
it wouldn't fit into available space.

*P*ot-likker hounds are a
shame to a hound man, but almost
every hound strikes a red fox that
is his match sooner or later, gets
worn out before the race is over,
gives up and comes pot-lickkerin'
into the fire. It happens.

But there are a lot worse things than pot-likkering to a fox hunter. Among these folks, the hound that wears the hardest name is the dog that is guilty of *cunning running*.

Called a "cuttin' dog," this is the hound that doesn't follow an honest scent but—guessing at territory, or the fox—takes a short cut to anticipate what foxes have done before. In other kinds of hunting this might be seen as a smart dog taking an advantage, but it's cheating to a fox hunter who expects his trustworthy hound to stay with the trail and keep to the evidence.

Since a fox race is all about endurance and perseverance to a trail, fox hounds are expected to stick to the scent and run as a pack, some fast or slow, but all honest. A "cuttin' dog" can lead young dogs off and confuse a race.

I used to hunt with a group of neighbors that was joined one night by a relative of one of them called Elmo. Elmo had brought his own fox-hound, 'Old Buckshot.' Buckshot was a pedigreed, Hedspath hound with a sharp yelp like a bugle, but sometime well into the race we heard that new voice out and away from the pack.

"That hound's cuttin'," one of my neighbors whispered to me. Two pup's voices followed the stray. Elmo wasn't paying attention because he was bragging about his son, who had just begun medical school up in Columbia. As the hounds got out of hearing, Elmo got on a roll extolling his son's brightness, his superb grades, and his race to become an MD. "Why, in four more years at Columbia I expect him to be my doctor." said Elmo.

About that time the dogs came in hearing, Buckshot leading the pack, the equally cheating pups behind.

"How's that for a fast dog?" asked Elmo triumphantly.

Fox hunters are polite folks and he didn't hear what one of them mumbled to me. . . .

"If Elmo's' boy doctors like his dog hunts, somebody needs to go there to that medical school and leash him before he ruins the whole damn pack," he said, "much less kills his own daddy!"

It was an odd way of telling stories but I found that in time, I could always slip in enough description and color to make it work for me, and for the magazine. Meanwhile, I spent a lot of time writing down the funny things that occur when you try to hunt one animal, using several others to do it. I had thought that I knew a lot about dogs, but I had twice as much to learn about trying to do anything with mules.

My own mule was called Banjo, because he was as white and tight-skinned as a banjo head. He was a good mule and carried me faithfully for several years, but like all of his kind, he was the most stubborn animal I ever tried to work with. This is one of the stories I wrote about him, back in the '70s. . . .

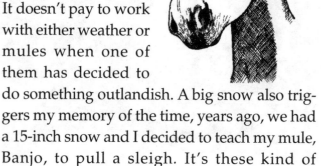

Every time a big snow comes I remember that it's nature's way of telling us it's time to play, not work. It doesn't pay to work with either weather or mules when one of them has decided to do something outlandish. A big snow also triggers my memory of the time, years ago, we had a 15-inch snow and I decided to teach my mule, Banjo, to pull a sleigh. It's these kind of thoughts, I believe, that have kept me from Alzheimers, boredom, and/or wealth.

In the first place, Banjo was a jumping mule, which is to say the kind of small mule that ageing coon hunters like to ride. Besides keeping you up out of the brush and saving all the miles of walking, a jumping mule goes over fences on demand so that hounds can be followed without hunting up gates to open. I had world's of fun riding Banjo and I decided that the children of my friends and neighbors needed to find out what fun we could have riding in a sleigh behind him.

The sleigh was an antique and though it was in good shape for its age—much like myself—I knew enough not to hook a jumping mule to it until he had mastered the business of pulling a less fragile load. The truth of the matter was that Banjo had never pulled *anything*, never having been in harness, but I was sure he could learn. After all, this wasn't rocket science here and I assumed that once a mule has learned to deal with a saddle and bridle, other encumbrances wouldn't be all that startling to him. It is this sort of assumption, of course, that caused the fall of the Roman Empire.

I did have backup, however, in the form of a friend, Steve Bryson, who was very good with mules, having had experience. Steve was the person who had taught me that a mule will be the most biddable, docile, and cooperative animal you could work with for 20 years in order to get your confidence so that he can kick you through the side of a pole barn. Steve, in short, was a master of mule reasoning.

The timely 15-inch snow gave us the inspiration to show Banjo his new job. The mule stood like an iron lawn deer while my friend harnessed him for the first time. Unlike a horse, a mule will wait until you make your intentions clear before he makes his own, and Banjo quietly absorbed the new sensations of collar pad, collar and hames, and the odd feel of leather across his crupper. We talked to him soothingly.

"This deep snow," Steve explained, "is perfect. He won't be able to get enough footing to do anything wild." For insurance, Steve tied a trip line to one of Banjo's front fetlocks and ran it through the hames. In case the mule panicked, Steve said, he could simply jerk that foot up and the mule would be unable to run.

He hooked the tugs to a single tree and that to a saw log. When everything was set, Steve took the lines and urged Banjo forward with a cluck and shake of the reins. Banjo gave a tentative step that brought everything up taut ,making it clear to the mule that he was hooked to something, and that further effort was expected of him. Banjo was willing. The very next step instantly turned into a bolt and I got to see Banjo, log, and Steve, go tearing off through the woods like something shot from a catapult.

Steve still had the reins, and I assumed was in control, but I couldn't help noticing he was taking steps like a wild turkey; just touching down to keep from flying. He yanked at the trip line. Banjo obliged by lifting that leg off the ground and showing us how well he could run on three.

What I could tell of them for a while was a comet trail through the still woods where the log was knocking snow laden saplings down, now and then a glimpse of my mule trainer strung out behind like a pennant, and the sounds of WHOOOOAAAAHHH BANNNNJJJJOOOOH. . . !

Like a fading train whistle.

Finally, Steve came back to join me, alone. We stood to listen while Banjo frailed that log over 80 acres trying to lose it. Steve had so much snow up his coat sleeves he looked stuffed, but he never lost that mule trainer look of dedication.

"Looks like we need a bigger log." said my friend thoughtfully.

"*Log?*" I said. "*Log?* I wouldn't trust that mule hooked to my truck if I ever wanted to see it again. Lord, I wouldn't hook it to a *courthouse*, if there was a snow on."

Steve had a look of nostalgia as we listened to the distant banging of trees and watched occasional puffs of dislodged snow shake from the tops of far away timber. I knew that something really hillbilly was going to be said.

"It's enough to make you believe in Santa Claus." said my friend, "If one mule can do that, imagine what a team of reindeer could haul around the country!"

When I wasn't working to finish some part of the log house, hunting, or entertaining company, I kept pecking away at the book. It wasn't easy to do this, even back in the woods, because at least a couple of times a week I would have to stop to make a trip to town for something I'd forgotten. In addition to that, people kept stopping by to see the new house and whenever the visit went past the middle of the afternoon I'd invite them to stay for supper. This took a lot of cooking and the first thing I knew we were out of something and I'd have to make another run to town. What made the company worth any amount of time I took away from the book, however, was the *visiting* my friends came for. These were the very people who had given up visits for TV so long ago and I was getting them back into old habits. A big sit-down dinner was worth fixing if the result was storytelling around the fireplace afterward. One of these stories, told on a winter night, has stuck with me for twenty years.

*H*owe Teague is a master storyteller. Given an audience of even one, if the person has an open mind, Howe will spin a careful line off his reel and see what he can snag.

His stories, told by anyone else, wouldn't cause a ripple, but in Howe's hands an audience gets fascinated by the nature of the lure.

Howe Teague was at my house last week, to play some music with me. We'd been sitting around the fire for an hour or so when we stopped to rest and wet our whistles. We had been playing *Rye Straw*, which Howe said always reminded him of Bunker, Missouri, and I sensed the hint of a story.

165

Howe never went at these things like a story-teller. He was more like a bystander reporting something funny.

"You ever notice anything odd about them phone poles they put up between Bunker and the Markoot Lookout?" he asked—then, shaking his head, "Well they're every different height you kin think of, like whoever put 'em up wasn't paying any attention to how tall they was supposed to be."

Howe went after the status quo. If he could hook you on the ordinary, he knew he could get your imagination.

"That was the first telephone line we got in this part of the country." Howe said, to establish the age of the story. "Now I don't know if this is so," he'd go on, "but I heard they hired a Bunker crew to put them poles up."

The story was now on familiar joke territory, Bunker being the Ozark equivalent of Poland as a source of hillbilly humor. Any story that called for incompetence was laid on Bunker. Howe would let that soak in; pretend to remember the details.

"They appointed old Farley Butts as the contractor. Well, Farley's dead now, and I wouldn't say a thing about him anyway because I'm some kin to him on my mother's side, but he wasn't no engineer, you know. All he did was tell them

Bunker boys what to do best he understood it. He says;

" 'Now boys, you see that pile of poles they brought a-laying there? And you see all them trees and all that brush growin' along the right-of-way? When I get back here tomorrow, I want all them trees and brush gone and not see nothing but a lot of crossbars sticking up out of the ground a 100 feet apart. Straight, level and plumb is what you need to remember.' "

Howe paused about here and lit his pipe, shook his head slowly, remembering something that was coming, squinting at his listeners to see if we had followed so far. Howe could get worlds of mileage out of a match, and puffing a pipe to life.

"He didn't think they needed no more directions than that." said Howe, "Didn't want to confuse them with too much facts, as they say." Howe's chuckle was always a *Hmm-hum-hummm*, around the pipe stem, sort of a grunting at his own memory.

"Well, he come back by there the next day and looked off down that right-of-way where it makes a big swag, and sure enough, them poles was lined up all right. He could sight across them crossbars like a rifle barrel but some of them phone poles was 30 feet tall and some was buried plumb up to the neck!"

When we had quit laughing at this ridiculous mental picture, Howe went on. . . .

"Well, Farley run down them Bunker boys a couple of miles down the road, still buryin' them poles just however deep, to make the tops level, and chewed 'em out good, you know.

"And the big looby who was runnin' the post hole digger says, 'Why durn it all Farley, you said level and plumb. You never said one damn mumblin' word about how HIGH!'"

That, of course, was the punch line and everybody roared at another Bunker joke, realizing there wasn't a word of truth in the whole story.

But then Howe did one of his little serious epilogue lines that made you wonder. . . .

"Course they had to reset all them poles, but they used the same holes, they tell me, and the first rain settled them in every which-a-way. You notice next time you drive by."

And that's the double-barreled flavor of a Howe Teague story, a joke you will laugh at despite its unbelievability, and Howe's own private joke that was, to him, even better.

"I told that one to the kids when they were little." he told me. "Don't you know, they never made a trip to Bunker but what they'd check every one of them phone poles every time!"

It was a good story, too damn good. I lived on the Markoot Road, 20 miles from anywhere and had to make that trip to Bunker twice a week. Even though I know he made it up from whole cloth, and assured as I was that it was told to make me laugh, I had the feeling I'd spend the next trip to Bunker measuring the phone poles with my eyes like some old fool, and hoping I could pass on that ridiculous story to somebody else. The real joke was, of course, on me. There are no phone poles between Markoot Lookout and Bunker, and never were.

Rectify *To Correct* —
   "My spellin' is so bad I get my wife to rectify my letters."

Reverence *To give credence to - To value* —
   "I don't reverence that TV weather man none."

Riddle   (1) *A colander -or- Sieve* —*"Leaks like a riddle."*
   (2) *To puzzle out something* —*"He riddled me out directions to Big Piney."*

Rifle *To despoil -or- To Rob* —
   "Best lock your car or some sorry rogue will rifle it."

Right Glad *Very happy* —
   "This baby's a girl and they're right glad of it this time."

Rile *To roil -or- Stir up* —
   "He's easy riled as a bee gum in cold weather."

Rogue *Gone wild - Untamable* —
   "Two drinks and he turns rogue on me."

Rue-back *To renege on a deal* —
   "I swapped him dogs last week and he's rued-back on his bargain already!"

Ruinate *Go to pieces* —
   "A house without no one in it will ruinate in a year's time."

Ruination *Destruction* —
   "Now that dog's the ruination of a coon, and he'll fight a circle-saw besides."

Chapter Nine

The Log House

Looking back over the years I worked on *The Glory Hole War*, I realize that despite the effort I was putting in on the book, I was spending most of my time catching up to the way of life that had pleased me so much and inspired the book twenty years before. I was story-hungry and would have to stop working at least once a day to write something down that a neighbor or a visitor had said or done. Sometimes these were just words that were dropped, like. . . .

> *"My granddaughter loves to drive the mower and I love to watch her mow, but I swear there's no field so big that she can't find some burly old donnick to harelip the blade on."*

Or a man commenting on how steep the bank of my pond was. . . .

> *"You wouldn't have to make but a step or so to dip your cods now would ye Mike?"*

Or a neighbor who I interrupted while watching TV one afternoon. He was watching Jerry Lee Lewis play the piano on some show. . . .

> *"Look at that feller clawin' it out of that piany,"* he said wonderingly, *"looks like he's one step ahead of a fit, don't he?"*

Or a comment made by a friend about his nephew who had taken up with a fast-lane crowd. . . .

> *"Well, you can't keep a squirrel on the ground can ye?"*

They were just odds and ends of words, but they were priceless in a way. Not even a tenth of one percent of Americans used these words anymore to say memorable things.

I was trying to capture it all before it got away; this colorful way of saying the most ordinary things that left the words ringing in my head. I was doing *The Glory Hole War* in Ozark dialect, having it narrated by a man who, like Zeke Dooley, used whatever words came to mind. It was great fun to do what felt natural, but reading over my chapters I began to wonder how a publisher might feel about paragraphs like this one by "Cooner" Watson, my narrator, describing his property to a land buyer:

> "Well, I own a pretty fair scope. I begin down at that big water oak against the road and run south to that big red barn yonder, under the hill. Thence west to where I corner against Crocker's, and the north line is kindly sygogglin' through timber because it's all on edge, ye see, but it fetches up and corners right fornent that bluffy part. Actual, part of that bluff is on me. Then you come east past where the road tears and just course it to here by the roof tree of my house."

It occurred to me that some editor from Lippincott would probably be stunned silly by this description, but I was so caught up in preserving the language that I wasn't going to worry about it. I was accustomed to my neighbors referring to anything on their property as being "on me," and using words like "tears," for forks; and "course," for sighting along. I just wrote what I heard and assumed that they'd figure it out.

It wasn't until a year or two later when I began submitting *The Glory Hole War* to editors that I realized I might as well have written it in Arabic if it was going to take a translator to make it readable. But for now I was collecting and putting away for safekeeping, the words and expressions my friends used and the stories that I heard every time I had company or went hunting with friends. Like this one told to me by a lady who had come out to see what a log house looked like from the inside and stayed to visit. . . .

"I had the Friends Of The Library Club over two weeks ago," she said, "and they were all making a fuss over Jeannie, my littlest one. You know, the one that's four?

"I'd dressed her up and told her Momma was having sort of a tea party. I told her I wanted her to be on her best behavior because this was a grown-up party, and she could do whatever she wanted as long as she didn't interrupt or show off.

"Well, she was as good as can be and I was just so proud of her. We were all sitting around discussing the work being done on the library, and I looked up and saw that Jeannie had gotten out her little tea set. She was offering tiny cups of water to the ladies. They thought that was really cute, and they were all pretending it was tea and sipping it. I thought it was pretty cute too until I realized there was only one place in the house low enough for that child to get her 'tea' water from."

We laughed together but I could see she had startled herself, telling me of all people this piece of embarrassment.

"Now if you ever tell that on me Mike Jayne, I'll hunt you down like a deer!" she said.

That threat didn't scare me much since Shirley wasn't all that good a shot, but still, I've waited 20 years to tell it. The reason I'm glad I have a good memory is that I was going to need it.

Just before Christmas of 1980 our log house caught fire and burned to the ground, taking with it everything we owned. There are no fire departments that far back in the woods and we couldn't save anything—as a matter of fact were lucky to save ourselves. We jumped off a second story porch onto the roof of our pick up truck and managed to get away from the blast furnace the house had became.

There is an old expression in the Ozarks that says, "Three moves are worse than a burnout." I can guarantee that this old saying is like, "all's fair in love and war," made up by somebody who has never been in either one. I don't intend to talk about that fire much but just want to say that if you have ever been through a flood, a tornado, or a fire, you will understand that people have to start over from scratch. In my case this meant letting go of about 42 years of putting things together so we could have them around us. It was the most naked feeling in the world, finding myself without a single record of our family's past, or one possession, besides what we escaped with.

Among the erased things of my life, neither more nor less important than any other, were the first ten chapters of *The Glory Hole War* and all my notes on Ozark speech.

What enabled us to survive was our friends who not only understood about burnouts, they also had the compassionate Ozark custom of seeing to each other. We were taken in and taken care of and then my old friends, The Dillards, got together once again to hold a benefit concert in Salem for us. That reunion was more meaningful than just the money it raised. It reminded me that I was still a part of something that was totally unburnable; my friendship with the Dillards.

Within two weeks, my old friend Lester Adamick came to visit us at the house where we were staying. He said that some friends wanted to help us rebuild our house and wanted to know where we would like it built.

One of the reasons I'm including this sad chunk of history in a book of funny stuff, is that this is also a book about the Ozark way of looking at things and the Ozark sense of humor. I was in the middle of grieving for my lost paintings, pictures, manuscripts, family heirlooms, all the little things we had collected, and I wasn't ready to talk about positive things yet. I told Lester that I didn't want to think about it.

Lester, who understood the old saying, "The more you cry the less you have to pee," was tolerant of my grief but impatient with it at the same time.

"You're not listening to me." he said. "We are going to build you a house and you'd better tell us where you want it or we're liable to put it in the wrong place."

Obviously, I was not going to be allowed to hang onto my grief around people like Lester and I soon took a hand in getting the house rebuilt. Not only neighbors,

but friends I didn't know I had, came in droves to help re-pour the old foundations and rebuild the giant fire-place. Despite myself, I drew up new plans for the house where the log house had once stood. Before I knew it my days were as full of the sounds of construction as when the log house had been going up.

Some of the people who helped were new to me. Their stories added a new dimension and would replace the notes that I had made about Ozark humor that no longer existed. One of the men from Lester's church group had a new moonshine whiskey story about his uncle John who had enlarged his own operation to the point where he had built a vat.

178

The final run from the still was poured from the vat into barrels for aging, as he told it, when . . . .

"Uncle John was up there on the board walk around that vat, stirring in some molasses to color it good and he fell in, paddle and all. Of course all of the fellers lit in to rescue him out of there. Uncle John fought them all off, best he could and he did manage to drown before they snagged him out, dead, but grinning.

They had a big service for him and he was cremated. Undertaker said he burned for three days with kind of a blue flame."

It was the finest therapy I could have asked for, and it never stopped. That story reminded somebody else of their relatives in Arkansas who, when they moved, took the house numbers with them so they wouldn't have to change addresses. This reminded one of the carpenters that his cousin, who upon learning from TV that most accidents happen within 20-miles of home, never came anywhere near his home and had his wife meet him at motels out of town.

I had never heard such a bunch of joke tellers in one place as in the rebuilding of the house, and no matter how dumb the joke, I found myself getting in better spirits every day. It wasn't only a matter of jokes, it was a matter of being around people who cared for other people. Helping a friend in need wasn't a matter of religious requirement either, since my friends were the oddest composite of religions you could imagine. They felt free to tell religion based stories to—and on—each other as well; an endless variety of religious jokes that made me remember what a hodgepodge of faiths are to be found in any Ozark town. It was a marvel of the culture that I was able to collect stories that had nothing to do with our own geography or background but had somehow just popped up when somebody opened a religious can of worms.

"Well, Jesus he was walkin' around one time," one of these stories began, "and here was a big crowd of people had a man hemmed up and they was fixing to stone him, you know, mash him to death with rocks. Jesus he says, 'Wait a minute here, you people, don't none of you'uns read scripture?' Says, 'It's wrote down right there in the gospels, let the one amongst ye who is without sin cast the first stone!'

"So that kind of stopped 'em, made 'em think, you know, but about that time here come a little woman out of that crowd and she just bustled right up there and picked up a big donnick and let it fly at that man they had caught up—like to brained him. And Jesus, he says, 'Mother, sometimes you just come awful close to pissin' me off.' "

That one opened the door to an Amish story, of all things. . . .

"Well, they was one of these Amishmens, lived up north around Hannibal or somewheres on the river, took his family down to St. Louis on a boat. You know, those people don't believe in electric, or owning a car, and do all their farm work with teams? Don't use toilet paper, only a cob and such as that. Well, he wanted to show his children all the sinful ways of the city. He figured that if they was to see all that vanity and waste and so on, they'd know what to avoid in life. Well, they put up at a hotel because they had to stay some'ers and didn't know anybody, and while the women folk were off lookin' at all the plunder in the gift shop, the old man, his eye fell on an elevator there in the lobby. He'd never seen one, you know, and he didn't know what it was for.

"Well, while him and his boys was watching, a little old lady come over in a wheelchair and loaded herself in there, and the three of them watched a big dial go on up to the highest number and stop, then directly start down again, and when the door opened, a beautiful young gal stepped out.

"This old Amishman looks at her and says to his sons, 'Boys, go find your ma and tell her to step over here a minute!' "

The laughter would be uproarious at one of these stories, and all the hammering and sawing would stop until we had our laugh out. There were even Jewish stories told, although there hadn't been anyone Jewish in Salem for years, and I don't think anyone was sure what Jews believe. Instead, they turned them into Scotch jokes dealing with penury since both nationalities were associated with that. One of the guys mentioned that he had known a Jewish man in the service who, he said, referred to non-Jewish people as 'genitals.'

I remember his attempt to capture Jewish humor....

"There was this Jew feller had a son and he wanted to teach him about life, just a little old kid, you know, maybe five year old, and he took and set him up on the mantle over the fireplace. Says, 'Now Hymie, jump off of there and daddy will catch you.'

"Well, the kid, he didn't much want to do it, but his dad says, 'Hymie, trust me, I'll catch you. Come on and jump into daddy's arms.'

"The kid never would do it, you know, but finally he done it. Just leaped right off there and the feller stepped back and BAM! That lad hit the floor like a sack of meal. Kid lights in hollerin' like he's killed, and he yells, 'Why didn't you catch me? You lied to me!'

"And his daddy says, 'Son let this be a lesson to you, don't trust NOBODY in this world, even your daddy!' "

It was amazing to me, to hear my Ozark neighbors telling ethnic jokes like this that had nothing to do with their own experience. It was sort of like finding a tribe of Wastusi who knew Polish jokes, or finding out that Eskimos really get off on Irish humor.

I've always been fascinated by people who remember jokes. I'm sure you've met one or two of these marvels of long term memory, who seem to know every joke they ever heard and one reminds them of another.

When I was in the service I met a lot of these boys, who would while away hours at sea, telling every Pat and Mike, moron, guy goes into a bar, shaggy dog, priest–rabbi–preacher, Polish, Italian, Negro, and Jewish joke, plus every one they had ever heard about drunks, in a marathon of funny concepts that seemed to have no end.

I used to worry about my own retentive memory because I couldn't remember more than one or two of the best ones, and them not for long. I decided some years back, however, that there wasn't too much wrong with my memory, it was just that the ones I did remember were told by someone who was really good at telling a story. As Andy Griffith used to say, "Some's got it, some ain't." I wouldn't remember a Texas joke unless it was told by someone from Texas who had an accent as broad as the state and made the joke memorable.

Which reminds me of one. . . .

Two school teachers met at a convention in St. Louis and were getting acquainted. One was from Texas and the other was from Massachusetts. The Texan was one of those good-natured El Paso people who can make any word a yard long, and he asked the Boston man, "Wheah did y'all gao to skewell?" The guy from Boston told him "Yale."

"Oh, Okay," said the Texan, and cupping his hands shouted, "WHEAH DID Y'ALL GAO TO SKEWELL?"

What I had started to tell you was, I have a feeling that 90 percent of a funny story is the teller. As we worked on the new house I got to hear some of my friends exchange stories about Dent Brother's hardware. That was because one of us had to make trips to Dent Brothers at least once a week for supplies. The three Dent brothers had inherited their father's hardware business and by 1981 had kept it going in pretty much the same fashion for 75 years.

Dent Brothers was located on the square, across from the courthouse, and embodied every element of small town hardware stores of the 30s when I was growing up.

Back then, hardware stores carried everything from horseshoe blanks to saddles. Every conceivable type of nut, bolt, washer and screw, stoves and their parts, every sort of tool imaginable, and literally thousands of tiny parts in tiny drawers that lined the walls and had to be reached with long ladders. I remember the thrill for me to be sent after something like a window shade pull, and while waiting for some old man to find the proper drawer, feast my eyes on the pocket knives in their glass case, the guns stacked in long oak cabinets, the bicycle accessories on display for me to wish I had.

By the time we were rebuilding my house, most of these old fashioned stores had been replaced by departments at more modern stores like Wal-Mart or Home Depot, but Dent Brothers had survived all the changes in merchandising and still carried everything the stores of my childhood had.

The three brothers, Pete, "Doc," and Bill, in descending order (Bill was the baby, being only 70 years old), continued to serve their community with the same things they had always dispensed, plus wit, humor, and a patient understanding of the Ozark customer.

I had always shopped at Dent Brothers. The time I decided to train my mule Banjo to pull a load in harness, I had gone into the store to buy some collar pads to keep the small mule collar from galling his shoulders. Bill was the brother who waited on me; he looked a lot like an owl, with heavy horn rimmed glasses and a forelock that always touched them.

"What color is the mule?" he asked me, deadpan.

Being new to both collar pads and mules I was dumbfounded.

"Well, he's white," I said, "but what difference would that make?"

"Dent Brothers," he informed me, "specializes in color coordinated collar pads. And by the way," he added, "can't you bring him in for a fitting? You only make a purchase like this once and we want it to be right."

It was the sort of thing that you weren't liable to hear at a Wal-Mart, even if they had sold mule collar pads. But this was the sort of thing that has kept people coming back for what, by now, must be over a 100 years.

*O*ne of my house builders told a great Dent Brothers story. . . .

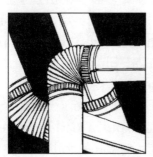

"I heard a good one on Doc." he said one day while we had stopped for lunch. "You know how ornery it is to cut stove pipe, well, Doc just hates it, says it's worse than bob wire to take a bite out of you, and he always tries to lay it off on Bill or one of the other fellers that works there. Well, a man come in and bought two or three lenths of it and had to have a half lenth to go with them. It was Bill's day to work in the shop room, and he was back there puttin' yard benches together, and here come Doc back.

"Says, 'Bill they's some damned old fool out here needs a half lenth of stovepipe cut.'

"And says, he seen Bill a-lookin' at him plum horrified, and he seen out of the edge of his eye that old feller that wanted the pipe had follered him back to the shop, out of curiosity, I reckon, and had heard the whole thing.

" 'Ol Doc, he was embarrassed, but never lost his wits.

" 'And this gentleman here,' he says, 'is going to take the other half!' "

Another man who had worked for the Dent Brothers for years, until he retired, told about the system of signals the brothers used between themselves, to clue some employees who had gone to wait on an old customer.

"Well, Bill, I think that's a W.P." Pete would call out. In Dent Brothers code that meant, "won't pay." And there were others; O.U.M. meaning, "owes us money." It was just an in-joke, but after a while it was also one everybody got to know about in a small town like Salem. Everybody, that is, except the brothers themselves who thought their code was private.

*O*ne time, my storyteller said, a man came into Dent Brothers to shop for some linoleum and took forever picking out something to suit him. Pete, figuring the man was going to go someplace else anyway, hollered out, "Joe, that's a W.O.T." and the customer, who had heard stories about the code, turned to Pete angrily. "I heard about your W.O.T. dammit." he shouted, "You think me lookin at your linoleum is a waste of time?"

"Why no sir," said Pete, thinking as quickly as he could, "W.O.T means the price is With-Out-Tacks."

These kinds of stories, true or otherwise, were the staple of Ozark conversation and I could always associate the story with the person who told it. Except in the case of the Dent Brothers and other local people who caused their own form of hilarity, most stories weren't original by any means, most of them going back a 100 years or so. Since the teller didn't know this, (most really good storytellers thinking that any story was real but needed retelling with familiar characters), the whole magic of hearing one of these depended upon the person who told it.

Like the pig story, which I heard from a fellow fox hunter who claimed he had heard this first hand. . . .

"I heerd old Vance Prater got his comeuppance the other day. He has a timber contract out by you and heads out there to cut sawlogs every morning. Now you know how that old boy drives anyway, couldn't drive a goose to water and takes both sides of the road. Well, the way I heard it, that lady works at the Bunker Bank, Fern Brown, she lives out near the Low Gap and ever morning she meets Vance on the road, both of 'em goin to work, and has to lay over for him. It's got so's they dodge each other about like bats on one of them big blind curves.

"Well, the other morning Fern come hellin' around one of them bends, and of course Vance was right in the middle of the road as usual and he had to cut a didoe to keep from puttin' it in the grader ditch, and she leaned out her winder and shouted, 'PIG!' loud as she could as she went by.

"Well, Vance, he was tuck a-back at that, you know. All the time they'd been dodgin' each other it had been pretty good natured and now she'd fell to blackguarding him.

"You know, Vance's kindly slow movin', and by the time he'd thought to yell back at her, she was gone. So Vance jerked his old rig back up onto the road and come around the corner, and there in the middle of the road was a Poland Chiny sow, had to go four-hunerd pounds, which if he'd of hit it, would have plumb salivated that old truck.

"Vance was telling one of the boys at the sawmill about it, says, 'Well, I'm sure proud I never lost my Christian raisin' over that.' Says, 'You don't know how close I come to yellin', 'Damn 'ol heifer yourself!' "

It was told so well, it didn't matter that I'd heard the Pig story told nearly 21 years before and that time told on a one room school teacher near Rolla. This is one of the most engaging things about Ozark stories; they all get a chance to be reborn with each new teller who adds his own two-cents worth and colors them up to suit his habitat.

You have to remember though, that like the weather starting at Winona, all these stories had to start someplace. One of the stories I'd heard that I still think is an original chunk of the Ozarks, is a story about Elmer McGee.

Don Knotts could have formed his Barney character after Elmer, a deputy constable in an Ozark town I knew, where the police chief was a mighty man whose reputation headed off trouble. Nobody messed with Chief Dewey, who was six-four with arms like hams, fists like a blacksmith, and eyes that were a chilling blue that sobered drunks up in a hurry.

His deputies consequently could be of any size or mental caliber because they represented Dewey. One of these was Elmer McGee, a skinny, strutting, comically officious little guy who carried a worn out pistol, and a blackjack so old the stitching was raveled. He had never used either one until the night of this story, told to me by Cecil Bates, the easy-going country boy who was his partner that night.

"You know Bessie Wright." Cecil told a group of us. "Her'n her sister are those big wooly gals you see hitchhikin' into town with bib overhauls and a pint in their hip pocket? Well, Saturday night Besssie was by herself and started a fuss at the tavern. Old Charlie was tendin' bar and he sent a boy over to tell us that Bessie had whupped up on a couple of loggers already and was running off all his customers, and for us to fetch Dewey, 'count of he was the only one she'd ever pay any mind to.

"Well, Dewey was home, sick with the flu, and Elmer he said we could handle it. I says, 'Elmer, they ain't no way you and me can handle Bessie Wright sober, much less drunker than Cooter Brown,' I says, 'that woman can pick up a tie log and pack it around, much less whup you and me!'

"But Elmer he said, 'She ain't bigger'n this here blackjack, son.' Says, 'If she won't listen to the law talkin', she'll listen to 'ol Blackie here!'

" 'Elmer,' I says, 'call Dewey.' Says, 'if we did down her, which I don't by no means believe fer a minute, the two of us couldn't wool her over to the jail, no more than a 40 foot bola constructor.'

"But you know Elmer, he'd never married and didn't know a thing about women, much less big wooly gals, and besides he was badge-proud and cockey with it, like a lot of little men are. He thought that blackjack made him Wyatt Earp.

"So into that tavern he went and of course I had to go with him, like a fool. Bessie, she was sittin' there at the bar lookin' in her beer, and Charlie, he was standin' back out of the way, lookin' nervous.

"Be damned if Elmer doesn't walk up right behind her and takes out that big old backjack, which no tellin' where it come from, Jesse James' grandpa maybe, and he says, 'Bessie Wright, you are under arrest fer drunken disturbance of the peace. Put your hands behind you because I aim to handcuff 'em.'

"Well, Bessie, she didn't even look up. She says, 'Elmer don't be messin' with me or I'll hurt you.'

"Boys! Before I knowed it, Elmer wound up and come down with that blackjack right top of her head! My lord, I thought, he's kilt her. But instead of the THUNK sound that blackjack should-a made, it jist kind of says FLUP! and birdshot come a-rainin' out of that rotten old leather and rattled agin' the mirror. Charlie, he went under the bar like a groundhog and I was thinkin' that was a pretty good place to be myself.

"Bessie, she looked up at the racket and seen us fer the first time. 'Boys,' she says real solemn, 'I ain't a-going to repeat myself to you little piss ants, leave me alone or I'll salivate the both of you.'

"Well, I believed her, and Elmer he was jist lookin' down at his blackjack kindly hangin' there like a sheep's tongue and it disheartened him so, he never thought about pullin' that old gun he had, which is a God's mercy because no tellin' where Bessie would have stuck the thing, and I says, 'Come on Elmer, we need to call Dewey.'

"So we went over to the police phone that hangs on the post out there by the courthouse, and done it; and pretty soon here come Dewey, madder'n a wet cat and lookin' like hell before breakfast in a ratty old bathrobe and a Vicks rag wrapped around his neck. He didn't even look at Elmer and me, jist strode through the door and up to Bessie and says, 'Bessie, you look at me good. I'm a sick man and I'm in no mood to mess with you.'

"Bessie, she'd set up straight when she seen Dewey and she listened to him with her head all hangdog, like some little kid caught in the cookie jar. 'Yes Dewey,' she says.

" 'Now you go over to the jail with these officers,' says Dewey, 'and you don't give them no more trouble or you'll have to answer to me in the morning.' Says, 'You'd ort to be ashamed of yourself, big growed girl like you, showin' your ass and actin' the fool!'

"So Dewey strode off and got back in his car, sneezing like a steam thasher, and that woman let us put handcuffs on her, and she come along with us meek as a lamb. But jist as we was coming abreast of the jail, she stiffened up and got in one last remark.

" 'Well, I'll tell you one thing,' she says, 'if you aim to benight me in that dirty jailhouse, you'uns are going to have to get me some Kotex.'

"That kind of took me aback, thinkin' she had carried on more like King Kong than a woman, but what poor old dumb bachelor Elmer says to her, beat anything I have ever heard. He kind of rared back all haughty and he says; 'Bessie, while you are in this jail, you will eat the same kind of breakfast cereal the rest of the prisoners eats!' "

These were the stories of home. Along with the knowledge of the deep friendships that had made it possible for us to survive they had given me a new grip on my purpose. I was going to write about the Ozarks, my neighbors, and my friends, because they were what I had learned the most about in my life.

S  Ozark Words

Sanction *Allow —*
   "Mother don't sanction whiskey in the house."

Scenery *A view or a picture of a view —*
   "That's a real actual scenery of the hog butcherin' works at Winony."

Scope *All the land you can see —*
   "I own a pretty fair scope of land, runs from here to the creek."

Shifting clothes *A change of clothing - lack of money —*
   "Buy a car? I ain't got shiftin' clothes."

Slay *To kill —*
   "I wait fer a hot day and use a brush hook to slay my weeds."

Sleight *A trick —*
   "They's a sleight to callin' up these fall turkeys."

Sorry *Worthless —*
   "That's the sorriest bunch of hounds I ever seen to hunt."

Spile *To spoil —*
   "Gimme that knife. I'll either make a spoon or spile a horn."

Squander *To fling at random —*
   "The left barr'l of that shotgun squanders shot."

Still yit *Despite that —*
   "He knows whisky'll kill him but he still yit drinks it."

Strenth *Strength —*
   "That boy don't know his own strenth."

Sull *To play dead -or- To be sullen —*
   "If he couldn't have his way, that child would sull fer an hour."

Chapter Ten

Home Fried Lies

I guess that everything I've told you up to now was meant to explain the reasons why I tell stories for a living instead of being a professional something or other, or being at least a responsible, salaried adult as my parents had hoped.

I have taken a lot of your time doing this, and it might seem sort of anticlimactic to tell you the rest, but I'd better do it anyway. I figure lots of people are like me, wanting to know the meaning of things the same way I like to know the meaning of words, asking kid-like questions about the importance of things such as: "Why do people in countries no bigger than a wheat field have different languages than the one next door to them?" and "What's so funny about being a minority group that if we didn't make up jokes about them, they would?"

I'd hoped that what I've established, so far, is that Ozark people are storytellers by nature and custom, and the language, by which these stories are passed on, is considerably more colorful than textbook English. I can hope too, that by this time you realize that truth is no more important to a good story than facts are to a Missouri weather forecast. The story about Ebo Walker, whose 160 proof corpse was able to, "resurrect two Jehovah's Witnesses, next plot over," is the epitome of an Ozark "Home Fried Lie." The awesome quality of the concept is what pleases our Missouri sense of humor; as Mark Twain showed readers a century ago with *Baker's Blue-Jay Yarn*. We know the story isn't true but we can't wa it to see how far the teller can go with it, and see what he has saved for a punch line.

At any rate, by this time I hope I've let you know how much I liked my home, valued my life, my work, and the people around me. But I have found to my surprise, that life can be as unpredictable as a fox hunt; where the rules change with every shift of the wind, every scent on the trail and every whim of the fox.

In 1989 I agreed to leave home, lay writing aside for a while, give up my hounds, and my mule, and my retired ways to go once more to play music with my friends, the Dillards. It wasn't my idea at all, it wasn't even the Dillards. It all came about in 1985, when Andy Griffith decided to revisit the little town he'd invented and he brought most of his cast members together for one nostalgic hurrah; *Return To Mayberry*.

It was a good trick, not because reunions had never been done on TV, but because the town of Mayberry, which had always been mythical anyway, was gone, and its former citizens were doing other things. The old cast was spread out like a coon hide, from one end of the country to the other.

Let me give you an idea of the logistics involved. . . .

The Mayberry exterior set on MGM's back lot had been torn down for 20 years, its buildings split up and used in a dozen other locations, and on other shows. The same things had happened to the interior sets at Desilu studios, everything mercilessly cannibalized into Hollywood's digestive tract.

Floyd the Barber, had died; Aunt Bee was in a nursing facility; and Opie was now a Hollywood director, rich, and busy with a dozen projects. He was nearly bald and no longer even looked like his character on *Happy Days*, much less Opie Taylor.

Briscoe Darling was directing films in Europe; sister Charlene was a film location expert for the Nevada Film Board; Rodney and Dean worked at Silver Dollar City in Branson, and Douglas had his own band in Nashville. Goober was a mainstay of the television program *Hee Haw* in Nashville, and Gomer was headlining in Hawaii, where he owned a macadamia nut plantation. Barney was fighting macular degeneration, and having to have his movie and stage play lines read aloud to him by a script girl. Ernest T. Bass was directing TV sitcoms. Thelma Lou and Helen Crump were both working in plays around the country.

Only Andy Griffith was readily available, despite the fact his pilot show *Matlock* had been picked up for a network series for the next season. He had busy times ahead. The reunion was Andy's idea and anything Andy really wants to do, usually gets done.

The little town of Los Olivos, in central California, was chosen as the location for the new Mayberry. Word went out to former cast members that we were going to recreate Mayberry one more time. It is a pretty good measure of everyone's genuine regard for Andy that nobody passed up on this chance to revisit a town that didn't even exist.

In the middle of January, 1986, I packed a suitcase, took a look around at the frozen woods of home, and said good-bye to the house and—though I didn't know it at the time—a way of life that is still way too good to be true.

All of us Dillards met at the airport in St. Louis and prepared to go back in time and become the "Darlings" again. The rest of the boys all looked the same but I had a big white beard that I had grown against the Ozark winter. I wondered if anyone would recognize us and if we would recognize the rest of the cast, but I needn't have worried.

The first person we saw was Maggie Peterson, who had played our sister Charlene. Seeing her plunged us back into that Hollywood world of make-believe. We were actors again—sort of. It was right back to Glenn-Glenn Studios to pre-record the music and read the script to see what time had done to our mythical Mayberry.

We were taken by van out to the set, a three hour trip from LA. It was there that the magic had been happening, for when we got out of our various vans, we were in the middle of the Main Street with the newly hatched little town of Mayberry gleaming before us in the sun. Andy's staff had done their homework. Los Olivos, California, had volunteered to become Mayberry, and the sets—from the courthouse to the end of the block—were false façades built in front of existing businesses. Andy's people had dug-up the old plans for the original set and everything was in its place; the barber shop, the grocery store, the Fix-It Shop, and most important, the courthouse, right where it belonged, all shining with new paint and looking like a childhood memory. All the cars on Main Street had North Carolina plates and across from the courthouse, up on a trailer, was the old Model-A truck that had first brought the Darlings to town. We were back.

All of us new arrivals stood looking at Mayberry, risen again like Brigadoon. We were speechless for a moment, and then here came Andy who was shorter, somehow stockier, and white haired. Along with him came a dozen people I didn't know (or didn't remember), except for Bob Sweeny, the director who had left the Andy Griffith show in 1967 to direct *Hawaii Five-O*. Bob was wearing hearing-aids in both ears and it gave me a strange kind of comfort. They had already been filming for a week, but Andy made sure he was there to meet everyone and greeted us all by our first names. He hadn't forgotten anybody and his eyes looked us all over lovingly, noting how much older, fatter, thicker, shorter, balder, grayer, we had all become, taking it for granted. Twenty years is a long time by any reckoning and he understood.

"Let's make this picture before we all die!" he said.

And of course, make it we did.

When *Return to Mayberry* aired the following May, a lot of people remembered the Dillards, including a lot of people in the music business. An agent approached Rodney about the possibility of all of us getting back together to do "a couple" of close-to-home concerts for the nostalgia crowd. We all thought about it for a long time because we were already busy in our own ways.

Finally, we decided the money was so good we couldn't turn that part down, and besides, the original Dillards hadn't been on tour together since 1964. We were curious to see if it would be fun to work together again.

In 1989, we went for it. Augmented by a dynamite musician named Steve Cooley, who Rodney hired primarily to be my ears, see that I was in tune, and keep time to his rhythm guitar—we went on the road again. Steve turned out to be a lot more than just a hearing aid for me. He became a rock of dependability, adjusting to all of us, while adding his own inventive dimension. Most important to me was the fact that Steve was funny, a quality that always works in a band. He never let me take my deafness seriously.

One time, when called over to re-tune my bass at a rehearsal he said, "Hi, I represent the Bluegrass Outreach Program To Aid Deaf Old Farts." I was definitely among friends.

The ancient—by today's standards—Dillards were back in business and the other guys were as hot as ever. Since my bass playing had never been what made me important to the Dillards, it was adequate, and the story telling still worked fine.

The four jobs turned into 40 and the 40 into 80. Before we were even sure we wanted to, we were doing concerts in England, Ireland, and Japan for people who had never seen *The Andy Griffith Show* but had listened to music we had played 25 years before. We were now appreciating the impression we had made on strangers when The Dillards first began.

One hundred thirty concerts later, in 1992, The Dillards finally disbanded. It was with the knowledge that anytime we wanted to, we could go back on the road and appreciate for ourselves the magic that Dillard reunions seem to have, one more time. For me it had been the best of both worlds. While on the road I would listen to stories told by other bluegrass musicians who came from mountain country much like our own. . . .

*D*on Stover and Bill Vernon were both storytellers of the old whipsaw school, which is to say that one would tell a story and that would inspire the other to tell one. Between them, they could come up with some of the most hilarious stories in Bluegrass, a music which abounds in humor.

One night, backstage at an awards ceremony, I got to hear these two get started on Bill Monroe stories. Bill Vernon had studied the workings of that irascible old man's mind for years, and Don had actually worked for him. I was listening to hard copy definitions of Monroe by two of the funniest and wittiest people I knew.

They had gotten around to Monroe's stormy relationship with his brother Charley, which with maturity got even worse.

"Lots of times they wouldn't speak for a year at a time," Bill Vernon said in an aside to me, and that cued Don Stover, who told about the time

they were starting out to do a show. ". . .and Bill was giving directions to the driver before we even got out of town. 'Turn right here,' he says, 'now turn left. This won't be much out of the way. Now go straight and turn left. Now, that house on your right, stop and let me out just a minute.' "

The next thing he knew Bill was knocking on the door of a house and Charley Monroe came to the door. Bill promptly swung his fist and knocked Charley flat on his butt.

"We heard him as he come back down the walk," Don said, "He was shoutin' over his shoulder, says, 'You've had that comin' for over a year.' And he got back on the bus in high good humor and never said another word about it to anybody."

Bill Vernon came back with this:

"Remember the time," he said, "when Bill got to thinking it was Christmas and time for good will to all men? He went over to Charley's with a ham under his arm, to make peace."

"Well, he went up to Charley's door and knocked and Charley's wife answered it. Charley was sitting in a lounge chair reading the paper and he didn't get up. Charley's wife was surprised and pleased to see Bill, of all people, because he and Charley weren't on speaking terms.

She said. 'Why Charley look here, it's your brother Bill and he's brought us a ham!' "

"And Charley looked up and said, 'Tell him to put the ham on the porch and get the hell off my property!' "

After hearing a story like that, I would go home to write it down. The next week I'd hear a home story from Salem, like the one about a man who was driving his son's Corvette up in St. Louis county and opened it up to 100 miles an hour, just for the thrill of going fast just once. A State trooper chased him down and pulled him over. . . .

"Now look," said the trooper, "this has been a long day for me and you don't look to me like the kind of guy who drives that fast all the time." Says, "Tell you what I'll do. You give me a reason I've never heard for trying to outrun me and I won't write up the paperwork on this."

The Salem man thought a minute and said, "Well, my wife ran off with a State trooper last month and I figured you was him, trying to run me down and bring her back!"

Although I loved the stories I heard on the road, I was connected by natural blood lines to the ones told by my Ozark neighbors, like the story told about Doc Dent who was claimed to have said at a church supper; "All us old, bald fellers have holes in our pockets so we can still run our hands through our hair."

It wasn't that the stories from home were so much better, most of the time they didn't even have a payoff line and you had to know the victim of the joke to appreciate it. There is a quality to Ozark stories that always reminds me that Ozark humor depends more on situations than words.

There is a Howe Teague story about some neighbors who cut wood for a living back in the 40s. At the time there was a war on and poor people in the country had a hard time getting gasoline and tires, even when they could afford them.

Howe said,

"Well, Everett and his two big boys had been a-cuttin' wood all day long on a big ridge back yonder where they just had to make the road as they went along. It was full of stobs and flint rocks as it was, and they'd have to stop every little bit with a flat tire. They'd been working since daylight and every time they'd take a load to the sawmill, they'd get a flat, you know, have to stop and get the jack out, and put a patch on the tube and pump it back up by hand, like you had to do in them days. You know, that was a lot of work, with wood on the truck, and by the time the day was over they was give out. They'd fixed eight flats.

"They dumped off the last load at the mill and was heading home at last, and they hadn't no more than turned off on their own approach up here, when they had another flat. Everett he says, 'Boys just let her sit here, it ain't but a mile to the house and we'll walk.' They was sick of them flats, you know.

"Well, they hadn't walked very far, when Everett thought about leavin' that truck, for they had a mortgage on it and hadn't had it long. He says to the oldest boy, 'Homer did you git the keys out of that truck?'

"And Homer, he never even looked up, he says kind of disgusted, 'No, but I hid the jack and pump good!' "

Stories like that are so timeless, and so Ozarkian in their nature that a book could be made of them alone. I don't trust a scholar to do that; someone who gets off on footnotes and bibliographies and cataloging things numerically. It isn't the kind of story to write down, (even though I just did), because the storyteller is missing and the reader would have to fill him or her in from his own experience. Howe Teague set the stage for his stories, gesturing and making points with his pipe, chuckling to himself, wrapping his characters in a wreath of smoke, frowning when they frowned. Howe's great talent was that he created visuals.

For my part, since I tell these things on stage, I can do the voices and fill in the background and it works. But writing these things down is a tricky business. The only reason I decided to try was that I'm afraid these home grown stories will otherwise become as lost in time as the tellers.

Some of these stories just fit into the flow of any gathering. . . .

At a family reunion, my cousin Ed told a story about my grandfather, who was bald as a rock, getting a haircut from a barber in Monroe City, Missouri. For the benefit of the barbershop loafers, the barber ran his hand over my grandpa's smooth dome and said, "Gus, this feels just like my wife's behind." Grandpa ran his own hand over his head thoughtfully and said, "You know, you're right."

Now to me, this is funny on several levels, enabling me to recall my grandfather, remember old time barber shops as centers of storytelling, and appreciate the joke itself, which turns out to be on the barber. To classify it as a type of joke and give it a number is to dehumanize the way we all make fun of life and of ourselves.

The truth of the matter, as in the case of Vance Randolph's collection of stories, *Pissing In The Snow*, was that these stories were considered off-color in that day, and had to be presented as having some intrinsic social value before they would be accepted in print. Consequently, the reader, by inference, was supposed to find them funny <u>and</u> educational. The reader had to put up with endless bookish notes explaining why the stories existed. This is a really effective way to hammer a story flatter than Kansas. The last thing an Ozark story needs is an antiseptic explanation.

This (of course) reminds me. . . .

I had a neighbor, who was a silversmith, repair a carved fox hunter's horn for me. The silver ring that held the lanyard had split when

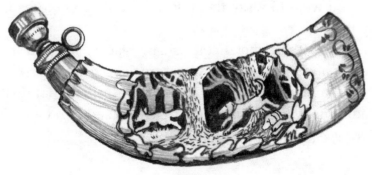

the horn swelled, and my friend Orville repaired the break.

"Now Mitch," he told me seriously, "if this ever breaks again, you just bring it back to me and I'll fix it for free. I stand behind all of my work."

Orville was adamant about this and wanted to be clear.

"As long as I'm alive, you can bring anything I've ever worked on back to me and there will be no charge for repairing it."

Having made this point so ponderously, he saw the humor of it and added;

"Of course if I'm dead, you're a *fucked monkey!*"

Try annotating and footnoting this piece of Ozark philosophy and you find yourself being both pretentious and ridiculous. It's just the Ozark way of underlining words.

Orville, I should add, is a master at using words that if you were to write them down, would have to be in italics.

"Now these metal cutting saw blades," he told me once, after cutting his finger, "are *forevermore* sharp!"

I have also heard a woman described—almost admiringly—as "*everlasting* ugly," and a hound as "*To hell and gone* loud on a trail."

212

I learned about this natural emphasis very early on. Back when I was teaching one room schools, I always had to find some sort of summer employment. One year I got a job writing feature stories for the *Salem Post*. The job didn't pay much, but the benefits were many and varied. I got to talk to old farmers who would explain things wonderfully. One old man pointing with pride at his house told me, "Hogs built that house!" I would think how funny that would look in print to someone not used to the way Ozarkers put things. Back in the 1930s, hogs provided the only cash a lot of people saw.

Another farmer said, "Back when I commenced a-farmin', equipment was always breakin' down and you couldn't get parts. There was cold winter days when the only thing that ran on this place was my nose."

Still another of these old subsistence farmers told me seriously that "Farming never has been what it used to be."

Writing for the paper in those early days was probably the best job I could have found to keep me centered on writing, but most of what I wanted to write I couldn't use, like the following story. I originally had sent it on to a friend because it was too funny not to write down and I knew I couldn't have it published anywhere.

It was frustrating to not be able to do anything with these stories besides tell them around a fire. None the less, I wrote this up, as if for a publisher and 40 years later I cleaned it up and sold it to a magazine. You can imagine the bowdlerizing I had to do.

213

A few years back a pair of bachelor brothers lived together down around Stone Hill, in the Ozarks. Like most brothers, they couldn't always get along. Whenever they would fall out with each other and weren't speaking they would bring the mailman into it. He was about the only person they saw every day and they'd wait at the mailbox to talk to each other through him. The mailman was a good-natured old fellow named Harley, who saw the humor of it and went along with this foolishness because he thought it was harmless and it, gave him something to tell at the barber shop.

A typical one of these quarrels, related by Harley, concerned Bill, who did the cooking and whatever house cleaning was ever done, and his brother Joe, who milked, fed the hogs, and did most of the outside work.

One day they were waiting by the mailbox ,and Harley knew they'd fallen out again.

Bill said, "Harley, tell my brother Joe that he is worse than ary hog to have around a house, and if he don't wash his feet today I don't aim to wash the sheets or cook another meal."

214

Joe looked at Harley and said, "Harley, you tell my brother Bill that if his cooking was half way clean I wouldn't have to be up in the middle of the damn night going to the privy with the running trots and come tracking in chicken manure."

This sort of thing went on for years, with each of the two old fools telling his side of the story through the mailman.

One day, when Harley stopped at Maudie's, the next neighbor over, he heard a story from the housewife that tickled him and he couldn't wait to hear what the old men would say.

Maudie had said her two boys, while on their way to school, took a short cut by the brother's barn and heard Joe preparing to milk his cow. Joe was talking to the cow, which he usually did, and told the cow, "I will give you turnips if you will give me milk."

The kids thought this was hilarious and setting the words to a tune, they ran off singing, "I will give you turnips if you will give me milk."

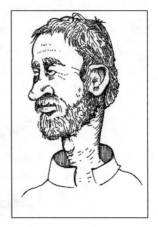

Joe, embarrassed to have been caught talking to his cow, wound up and threw a turnip at the kids. At the same time Bill was stepping out of the house to see what all the racket was about and caught the turnip right between the eyes. The children, of course, told their mother about this when they got home.

The mailman expected Joe and Bill to be waiting at their mailbox, and they were. Bill had a knot the size of a goose egg on his forehead.

Bill lit into it first. "Tell my brother," he said with dignity, "that he is a low–down–sneaking rock–throwin' son-of-a-bitch and if he don't apologize for near braining me, he will do his own goddam cookin' from now on."

Harley did his best to keep a straight face, which he said wasn't easy, watching Joe's as he heard Bill out. His reply, thanks to Harley, is still quoted in that part of the country whenever families fall out.

"Tell my brother," he said, "that it wasn't no rock, 'hit was a turnip and he can't talk about mother that way. And fur as eatin' his cookin' goes, I'd druther strap on a tin bill and pick shit with the chickens."

I am always thankful that I have written a lot of letters to friends who have saved them over the years and it has paid off big time. I seldom wrote a letter after I came to the Ozarks without including pictures, a clipping, several stories, some of the words I was learning, or things about folks I'd met.

I had deposited a large piece of my history with friends. After the log house burned, these friends began sending these things back to us, knowing that anything is valuable when you have lost everything else. Records we had loaned, books, pictures by the box full began to arrive in the mail and Jimmy Butler set a cardboard box aside for us to keep all these reminders of our former lives.

What follows is as near as I can get to taking you home with me to listen to people talk. I started writing down these wonderful ways of putting words together back in my teaching days, when I noticed that children put color into their descriptions as earnestly and as naturally as their parents did. Despite any of the other changes that might have affected Ozark life, people still use visual adjectives and remain folks who "see what their sayin'."

T·U·V· Ozark Words

Tears (Rhymes with Hairs) *Forks - divides —*
"*Just over the hill yonder where the road tears, bear to the left.*"

Touchious (pronounced techious) *Hard to please —*
"*That girl was raised touchious and she ain't improved.*"

Tole *To tempt in, to tantalize with something —*
"*These here wounded rabbit calls will tole in a fox ever time.*"

Tote *To carry —*
"*He's worth about what he kin tote on his back.*"

Tush *Tusk —*
"*These here wild boars got tushes long as yer finger.*"

Tutor *To spoil —*
"*She tutors that boy over all her other kids.*"

Umbrage *Offense (to take) —*
"*Any out of the way word, she'll take umbrage and fly mad.*"

Unthoughted *Unintentional —*
"*He left out in a hurry and unthoughted, left the gap open.*"

Use-Using *Make use of - inhabit —*
"*Ma won't cook a fish that uses in muddy water*"
"*The deers been using that alfalfa field.*"

Use in *-or-* **Use on** *Primarily, to feed —*
"*These deers are using on acorns. Them ducks use in mud.*"

Varmint *Vermin, i.e., nongame animal —*
"*Polecats is natured like a skunk, but they are a
nimbler varmint.*"

Vilify *To curse -or- demean —*
"*No man's goin' to stand there and hear his daddy vilified!*"

Chapter Eleven
Words With The Bark On Them

Contrary to what many people would think, most Ozark expressions aren't intended to make the listener laugh, but to make statements to other Ozarkers in terms they will recognize. They are sort of an in-language shared by folks who have always spoken in word pictures because these are more graphic and memorable; it's an almost inherited trait. A good illustration of this is the Ozark circuit judge who advised a lawyer entering a plea before him; *"Counselor, that dog won't hunt."* Meaning that his presentation was legally out of bounds. He would never have said that to a big city counsel, because the man wouldn't have known what he was talking about. Here are a few Ozark expressions that may need a little explanation, but in most cases, say whatever it is more clearly than most of us are apt to do in a conversation. . . .

HE'S POOR AS A WHIPPOORWILL
—skinny—

THAT MAN COULD WASH BOTH HANDS IN A GUN BARREL
—skinnier—

I'VE SEEN MORE MEAT STUCK TO A CHOPPIN' BLOCK
—skinniest—

HIS EYES ARE AS CLOSE TOGETHER AS A FISHIN' WORM'S
—Since worms don't have eyes, this is one of those ridiculous exaggerations we are known for—

GUESS I'LL DANCE WITH WHO BRUNG ME
—A way of saying you intend to stay with your
brand of car, political party, or barber—

THAT MAN SINGS FLATTER THAN
PISS ON A PLATE

EVERY FOX SMELLS HIS OWN HOLE
—Everybody knows where he belongs—

SHE LOOKS LIKE A HAY BALE
WITH THE TWINE BROKE
—Really obese or startlingly pregnant woman—

THAT'S A LONG SHOT WITH A LIMB IN THE WAY
—usually refers to an unlikely chance
of something happening, applied to weather,
political candidates, or a proposed marriage—

ONE STEP AHEAD OF A FIT
—Someone very excited or about to
lose his/her temper—

SO POOR THEY ATE THE WALL PAPER
—Wallpaper paste used to be made with flour and
mice would sometimes eat it—

YOU CAN'T FALL OUT OF A WELL
—Things can't get a bit worse—

221

LOOKIN' AT HER IS LIKE SMELLIN' WHISKEY
THROUGH A JAILHOUSE WINDER
—An out of earshot compliment about
a good looking married woman—

Ozark descriptions for ugliness never settle for the fact, but supply helpful words to make the adjective memorable:

THOSE GIRLS HAVE HAIR ON THEIR BACKS
AND LIP TATTOOS

IF YOU LIFTED UP ONE ARM, TWO BATS
AND A WHIPPOORWILL WOULD FLY OUT
—Mountain girls from the jillikins—

THAT MAN IS UGLY AS A GOUGE

HE'S UGLY AS HELL BEFORE BREAKFAST

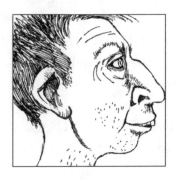

SHE'S SO UGLY SHE'D MAKE A TRAIN TAKE A DIRT ROAD

SO UGLY THEY HAD TO PUT A POKE OVER HER HEAD BEFORE THE BABY WOULD NURSE

Religious brands aside, Ozarkians are generally believers in God. Like the rest of their surroundings, they tend to take him for granted and talk to him, as in these expressions:

GOD, IF YOU'LL COME DOWN THROUGH THE ROOF TO HELP, I'D PAY FER SHINGLES.

IF GOD HAD MEANT LIFE TO BE EASY, WOULDN'T BE NO REPUBLICANS.

GOD DIDN'T USE NO EAST [yeast] WHEN HE BAKED THAT BUNCH.
—Meaning he didn't intend for them to rise, or do better—

Another of the terms that Ozarkians can't leave alone is the condition of stupidity. Descriptive words vary to cover the bases between simple ignorance, *"ignorant as a fishing worm,"* to mental deficiency, *"two bits short of a dollar."* Terms for real retardation are usually funny but gentle in nature, like the first three of the following:

ALL HIS DOGS AIN'T TREED

HIS BREAD AIN'T DONE

THAT POOR FELLER IS ABOUT
A BUBBLE OFF LEVEL

HE DON'T KNOW C'MERE FROM SICCUM!

IF HE WAS ANY DUMBER YOU'D
HAVE TO WATER HIM

SHE'S DUMBER THAN A BARREL OF HAIR

ALL HIS CORN'S NOT PICKED

SHE AIN'T GOT THE BRAINS
GOD GAVE TURNIPS

SORE AS A FLEA ON A CHALK DOG
(or IRON DEER)

HE DRINKS HIS OWN BATH WATER
—Believes his own lies—

HE LIES SO MUCH SOMEBODY ELSE HAS TO
CALL HIS HOUNDS

I WOULDN'T BELIEVE HIM IF HE SAID
MEAT WILL FRY

HE OUT MARRIED HIMSELF
—Married above his qualifications—

HE SHOD THE HORSE ALL AROUND
—Married four times—

I'LL SLAP A FART OUT OF YOU BIG AS A
LOAF OF BREAD!

I'LL KICK YOUR ASS LIKE PATTIN' [clapping]
FOR A SQUARE DANCE

EVERY OLD CROW THINKS HIS ASS IS
BLACKEST
—put-down for a braggart—

225

My favorite Ozark word shadings are the ones we use to describe people who have had too much to drink. Back home no one is allowed to just be drunk.

HE'S DRUNKER THAN COOTER BROWN

THAT MAN IS DRUNK AS A BICYCLE
(Or A FIDDLER'S BITCH, or A POW WOW)

HE SPENDS SO MUCH TIME DOWN HE KNOWS
FOLK BY THEIR ANKLES

HE GETS SO DRUNK HE HAS TO HOLD ONTO
THE GRASS TO LEAN AGAINST THE GROUND

HE JUST GETS A BIG JUG AND DRINKS TILL THE
WORLD LOOKS LITTLE

OLD FARLEY HAS HAD HIS BILL TOO DEEP IN
THE JAR

I DO BELIEVE HE'S DRUNK UP TILL WEDNESDAY

*THAT WOMAN BRINGS HER OWN WEATHER
WITH HER*
—Ill-natured—

THEY BROKE HIS PENCIL
—Didn't re-elect him—

HE LIVES OUT IN THE JILLIKINS
—Wild country—

WILDER THAN A BEE GUM
—Hive full of bees—

WILDER THAN A COYOTE
—Said about something usually placid—
"You can't gig these frogs; they're wild as coyotes"

CRAZIER THAN A BOX OF RECTUMS

The miserly or tight fisted have a special place in Ozark terminology, since stingy people make poor neighbors in lean times.

THAT OLD BOY'S TIGHTER THAN
DICK'S HAT BAND

SO TIGHT YOU COULDN'T DRIVE AN ICE PICK
UP HIS ASS WITH A POST MAUL

TIGHTER THAN BEAVER HIDE
—They are hard to skin—

HE WOULDN'T GIVE A DUCK A DRINK IF HE
OWNED CURRENT RIVER

HE WOULDN'T GIVE YOU A BUCKET OF WATER
IF HE WAS ON FIRE

HE WOULDN'T GIVE THE TIME OF DAY IF IT
WAS RAININ' CLOCKS

HE WHIPPED THAT FELLER LIKE A STEPCHILD

IF A GUN SHOOTS STRAIGHT, DON'T MESS WITH
THE SIGHTS

228

THAT MAN'S THE LITTLE END OF NOTHIN'
WHITTLED DOWN TO A POINT
—He doesn't amount to much—

THAT'S SMOOTHER THAN A SCHOOLMARM'S
WHOOSIS
—Usually whiskey—

SLICKER THAN DEER GUTS ON A DOORKNOB
(OR PUMP HANDLE)

I'D RATHER STRAP ON A TIN BILL AND PICK
SHIT WITH THE CHICKENS
—Referring to demeaning work—

THAT'S BARN CLIMBIN' WHISKEY
—Coarse or badly refined moonshine—

BOTTLED IN THE BARN WHISKEY
—Humorous term for moonshine,
based on "bottled in bond"—

THOSE BRUSH ARE SO THICK YOU COULDN'T
COCK A PISTOL IN THERE

HELL'S SO FULL OF LAWYERS THEIR FEET ARE
STICKIN' OUT THE WINDOWS

*YOU COULDN'T TURN ME OVER WITH A CAINT
HOOK IF I WAS DEAD!*
—A 'cant' hook is a lever for rolling saw logs—

*COULD STAND FLAT FOOTED AND
MATE WITH A TURKEY*
—Description of a short man or a big mosquito—

*HE'D HAVE TO STAND ON A WASHTUB TO LOOK
AT HIS PECKER*
—Another outrageous description of shortness—

*HE'D SCREW A ROCK PILE IF HE THOUGHT
THERE WAS A SNAKE UNDER IT*
—Typical exaggeration of *"He'd screw a snake if it had
handles," "He don't have no culls, comes to his
tallywhacker"*—

*THAT OLD BOY GETS AROUND LIKE SPIT ON A
STOVE*
—Describing someone square dancing—

*I'D LIKE TO GET MY CLAWS IN HER FLANKS AN
MAKE HER DRESS TAIL POP*
—I'd like to square dance with her—

HE GOES LIKE HE WASN'T JOINTED
—Square dancing—

*YOU TRY TO REMEMBER THE NAMES OF YOUR
FRIENDS AND LOOK FOR A PLACE TO PISS*
—A man's description of old age—

*THAT ENGINE KEEPS BACKFIRIN' . . .
IT'S JILLFLIRTED SOME WAY*
Jillflirt is an Ozark term for a woman who passes gas involuntarily because of an injury involved in giving birth.

THAT HOUSE SETS ALL WONKY- JAWED
This word for "crooked" is also applied to lumber, cars with broken springs, fence gates, or even the way people walk; just as the term, *"HUNTIN' POSSUMS,"* which refers to a tilted headlight, can also refer to a cast eye; *"WONKY-JAWED"* and *"SI-GOGGLIN"* are examples of handy made-up words that fit almost anything twisted or "yaunched" out of shape. A good example;
*"I yaunched my back some way and I've been walkin'
wonky-jawed all week."*

TOO FAR AND SNAKEY
Originally used to describe reluctance to go to a wild, remote place, I have also heard it used humorously to describe avoiding formal religion, a higher education, or even an involved concept:
*"I'd like to vote independent, but that Ross Perot is just too
far and snakey."*

231

HE/SHE'S A YEAR OLDER'N CORNBREAD
(Or DIRT, GOD, SIN , TREES, ADAM'S PET
MONKEY, SMOKE)
—description of an old person—

HE WOULDN'T BE SATISFIED IF YOU HUNG HIM
WITH A GOLD ROPE
—Usually said about young ne'er do wells, but used
humorously for anyone who can't be pleased—

YOU CANT KEEP A SQUIRREL ON THE GROUND
—Usually applied to limiting a child's freedom
but sometimes referring to adults who don't
fit the Ozark mode—

HIS MONEY WON'T LAST TILL IT'S GONE
—A spendthrift—

I'LL WARRANT YE, HE TELLS YE A THING, IT'S
THE WORD WITH THE BARK ON IT
—Not made up, but the truth—

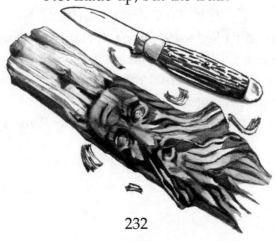

MOTHER-TONGUE

AND THE HAND WHITTLED WORDS

A long time ago, someone being asked to describe just what constitutes Ozark English came up with the expression "MOTHER-TONGUE"—meaning inherited language. As I have said elsewhere in this contrivance, I was always amazed that children in the first grade of one room schools often had a unique knowledge of words so long obsolete that they sounded quaint; like *"contrivance"* that refers to anything put together in an odd way, like; *"That woman's odd-turned, she's a regular contrivance."* No one who has really given it a lot of thought, would write an essay that tried to capture either Ozark language or humor without adding our "whittled" words. ("Whittled" words are the Ozark translation of unfamiliar words heard on television or on the radio or from conversations with someone who uses dictionary English.) These new words startle us but nonetheless impress us enough to get our nerve up to use them ourselves. What's funny happens when we attempt to use the word the same way in our own conversation, tossing it off as if it were natural vocabulary. Unfortunately, most Missourians (and all Ozarkians) hear what they expect to hear and when we try out a new word; what we come up with are "whittled" words, based on what we thought we heard. This enables us to come up with things like, *"that table is as stout as the rock*

233

of Ge-Gabriel!" or, *"they ought to put that Clinton feller on a liar detective."*

You have to understand that Missourians are free enough with ordinary language. In the northern part of the state we call someone named Howard, *"Haired,"* and Mildred, *"Millard."* We say, *"feesh,"* instead of fish, and *"warsh,"* instead of wash. In the Ozarks we turn stuff around when it suits us; say, *"tar,"* for tire (and vice-versa;) *"far,"* for fire; *"piller,"* for pillow. We also turn a lot of words that end in *"a"* —like "Ezra," into *"y"* or *"ee"* sounds, calling people *Ezry,* or *Marthee,* or *Alvee,* or *Berthy.* Instead of "you betcha!" we say, *"you betchee!"* We do it the other way around, too, just to be consistent and call Missouri, *"Missoura"*— and an ice-cream sundae a *"sunda."* We don't try to correct mother-tongue much, and when we do, usually mess it up worse. Except for *Missoura,* of course, which sounds so much more natural most natives pronounce it that way. When attempting to be correct (knowing that *"piller"* is basically wrong for pillow, and that *"holler"* is just mother-tongue for hollow), we attempt to fix up words like "bank teller," which I actually heard a guy change to *"bank tellow."* We also treat all words ending in "s" sounds like plurals; *"Do you have any license to hunt?"*—*"No, I don't need them."* *"Have some more of these molasses,"* *"these lettuce,"* *"them measles,"* and *"those arthuritis"* are all good Ozark terms to an Ozarker; the word lens is plural so if he loses one out of his glasses or a headlight, he is missing a len.

In other words, in speaking ordinary day-to-day English, we have speech habits that confuse just about everybody. But when you expose somebody from the Ozarks to a brand new word, their eagerness to say it right is often their downfall. The word *"Afghan"* sounded so sloppy to an old lady I knew that when I asked her what she was working on, she told me; *"I'm a-crocheting me an african."* She later topped that by telling me that she had a son, who raised *"Black Anguish cattle."* I figure that both words she chose just sounded more precise to her. Another Ozarkian who I met after I'd been gone a long time, told me that her oldest son hadn't been accepted into the Army because he *"couldn't pass mustard,"* but was now a *"highway petroleum."* I guess passing mustard isn't a qualification for Missouri troopers.

Where "whittled" words really get hilarious is in the area of medical terminology, which is hard enough for most of us, but to the old time Ozarkian, it's nearly gibberish. I ran into a lady on the street in Salem, Missouri, and asked about her husband. She said, *"He ain't no good."* Which might have been true, but her meaning wasn't criticism. She was only saying that he had been sick. *"They've been tinkering with Willy over to the hospital,"* she told me, *"and they say he's had a serbal hermage of the heart. For a while there they had to put him on auction."* This translates to a cerebral hemorrhage, (which she moved to the heart for handiness sake), with a reference to oxygen to show me that it was serious. A less informed person than me wouldn't have known whether to send a get well card or make a bid on Willy.

Other common ailments in the Ozarks are *"very close veins"* and *"fireball chewmers,"* which will put the sufferer *"under a doctor"* for no telling how long. The treatment for one lady I heard about included the doctors *"feeding her inconveniently,"* which I leave to your own imagination.

Ozark "whittled" words aren't limited to medical terms or even large words. A man I had traded coon hounds with told me that he had paid $500 for a dog. When I said that $500 didn't sound like much for a coon hound he said, *"T'wasn't a hound, 'hit was a dog fer my wife, one of them Cockerel Spaniards."* Another man told me that his preacher son had moved to the city and was now a member of *"The Salivation Army."*

I think the best of these "whittled" words was said by my neighboring woodcutters, who, thanks to television had heard of the *Guinness Book Of World Records*. The father and his son were delivering a cord of fireplace wood and saw a wild turkey gobbler standing in the road near my house. The son snatched a shotgun out of the window rack and, as he said, *"blowed his head off."* When the boy went to pick it up, however, the turkey flew. *"Now that,"* said the boy, *"should be in the World's Book of Genius."*

"Naw son," said the father, *"that ain't what they call it, it's the World's Book of Genesis."*

The "whittled" words are fun because you never know when a new one will turn up; as long as we keep coming up with new terminology and computer language there will be some Ozarkian to do something alarming with it. Like an old ginseng digger told me one time, *"these small town papers don't have much inflammation."*

QUOTED ODDMENTS FROM HERE AND THERE

One of the things I've always wanted to put in a book like this is a collection of things people have said that were important for some reason, whether they made sense or not.

When I was younger I was a great admirer of Henry Thoreau, who said a lot of pithy things like, "Beware of any enterprise that requires new clothes" and "live simply so that you can conduct life on your own terms." I still think that Thoreau was a sensible man, but I sure wish he had written down more of the insights and witticisms of his time as reflected by people he knew. I have a suspicion that no matter how smart you are, you have to have other people's input to put your own ability to absorb knowledge to the test.

When I left the Ozarks to travel with the Dillards, I learned something important. I found out that the Ozark knack for using word pictures to capture something isn't unique—only concentrated by a way of life and a language preserved by remoteness. In meeting and working with people from all over the country I was to find out that colorful speech is more the property of good listeners than anything regional; people who have taken the time to remember something said well, apply it to their way of thinking.

When the Dillards began to work a lot, we began to meet people who, like ourselves, had brought something of their own genetic and cultural background with them into show business, and I began to make notes. Since the William Morris Agency, who represented the Dillards for years, had no idea what to do with us, they tried putting us out like bait to see what part of the market we'd catch. Some of these bookings like, *The Judy Garland Show*, a night in a Las Vegas lounge, and an appearance on *Playboy After Dark* were so obviously a mismatching of fishing equipment that they became hilarious. The Dillards in tuxedos but barefooted, The Dillards on *Hollywood A Go Go*, The Dillards and Bill Cosby paired up in Cleveland, Ohio's 'Le Cave.' At one point we were even booked at the 'Hungry i' in San Francisco with Professor Irwin Corey for a week—the single worst combination of conflicting personalities I can remember, unless it might be the time we did a fair date with the Marquis Chimps. The benefit of these random and ill advised bookings was that we met a wildly diverse bunch of people we would have never run into playing Bluegrass music for Bluegrass lovers and I made notes of interesting comments these folks made.

We also found out by tackling these jobs once, which ones to avoid in the future. We not only changed agents a number of times in this learning process, but we developed a 'Pro' work ethic we could live with. We learned NEVER rules, like:

Never work on New Years Eve. (People who go to clubs that night haven't been invited to a party and are going to be both literally and figuratively pissed.)

Never try to work for an audience who didn't pay to see you in particular.

Never play a place where groping and drinking are the audience's primary agenda, and;

Never play anyplace where you will be asked to sing happy birthday to anyone, including the President. (People didn't pay to hear you pander to somebody's ego.)

It was a very good time to be in Hollywood for the Dillards, because we needed to see it and put it in perspective. For me in particular it was a chance to listen to speech and different expressions from every part of the United States. Though Californians themselves had no accents that I could figure out, they used words so strangely that I was in awe. I remember being stunned by one of our early landladies remarking, "I put my cat on kitty leapers to pep him up and now he's so ballsy he goes out every night and comes home wasted."

Teenagers had vocabularies that amazed me and were the first kids I had ever heard use big words like 'fabulous' or 'mordant' to describe movies and were the first I'd ever heard describe Bluegrass music as 'cool.' They had adjectives like 'dufy,' which meant dumb; 'boss' which meant good; said, 'far fuckin' out,' a lot; said, 'you know,' fifty times in a sentence, and expressed disbelief as, "Bag it, Stephanie, I am soooo sure!"

But the native's language didn't interest me as much as the hodgepodge of different people who had come to LA, dragging their cultures behind them like the Dillards towing our one-wheel trailer. People from everywhere had invaded the state. The mechanic that worked on my car was from France and dazzled me with words about ailing parts, like, " Eat ees thee shock automateek." or "Your probe-lem ees eeentek money-fold." I have tried to remember these things for whatever they might be worth. The truth of the matter is that a collector can no more stop accumulating stuff than a pack rat and what follows is a crusty, home-cured sample of what people said that mattered to them.

"This club of the Everly's will open new doors for you."
—NORMAN MALKIN
(The Dillards first manager)

"We'll put you guys in the Folk room and have the audience snap their fingers instead of applauding."
—DON EVERLY – Everly Brothers
(on hiring the Dillards for his new club which lasted a month.)

"I don't care what you're drivin', it's still a thousand miles across Texas."
—EARL SCRUGGS – (to Dean Webb on tour)

"Eastern Airlines could break an anvil."
—GRANDPA JONES
(speaking of musical instruments demolished)

"I never heard of one of these things backing into a mountain!"
—GRANDPA JONES
(upon being asked why he always flew in the very back of airplanes)

"I've got a grey cat that looks the most like a panther as anything you've ever seen!"
—DOC WATSON
(Who was born blind)

"Oh Dad's always taking that stereo apart, he can't
get it to suit him."
—MERLE WATSON
(Doc's son)

"Let's just run through it once and see how it feels . . .
and by the way roll the tape just in case "
—ARLO GUTHRIE
(recording his Dad's songs with The Dillards.)

"I don't believe in fancy, big name instruments. Get
the tone and leave the rest alone."
—BILL MONROE

"Now if you'll come up here and hep my driver start
that car, I'll jist set back here and honk your horn for ye."
—BILL MONROE
(addressing impatient motorist)

"Now in a car wrack you might get all tore up, and lay
there and suffer. But in one of these plane wracks, it's
POW! It jist tars the hinges off and there ain't enough
left of ye to bait a fish hook."
—JUNIOR SAMPLES
(explaining to his wife Grace why flying was the best
way to travel.)

"Mitch, you're from the country, come and look at this thing they gave me. All my fuckin' bugs are dead!"
—DICK CLARK
(looking at an ant farm – a gift from a high school)

"I think it's rude to interrupt a gospel number. Some people don't show any respect for sacred music."
—BILL YATES
(bass player for the Country Gentlemen, on bodily throwing a drunken, quarreling couple out the door of The Shamrock Club in Washington, D.C.)

" 'And The Hogs Eat Him?' Are you serious, is that really a song?"
—BILL COSBY
(working with the Dillards in Cleveland)

"Don, I'm going to whup you at this, you hateful puke! I'm going to whup you if it hare-lips the pope!"
—ANDY GRIFFITH
(playing darts on the AGS set with Don Knotts.)

"I always think of a motor home as meals on wheels"
—JIM CROCE
(arriving hungry while I cooked supper)

"It costs like hell to learn."
—A CLARENCE WEBB Saying
(Dean's dad)

HUGH HEFFNER: "Barbie, meet the Dillards!"
THE DILLARDS: "HI Barbie."
PLAYBOY AFTER DARK

"Guys, I know there's no money in this, but it will
open new doors for you."
—MICKEY SCHATZ
THE WILLIAM MORRIS AGENCY

" I 'd like to be someplace else."
—RODNEY DILLARD
(at a concert for a Lyndon Johnson appearance, seeing
the row of secret service snipers on roofs surrounding
us)

"I don't know why a doctor would want to get another
doctor to work on him—that's like settin' a beagle dog
after a rabbit and then follerin' the beagle."
—ALEX EMORY, Salem farmer

"What you boys need is some nice cravats. We're tryin'
to give this place some class, here."
—VEGAS LOUNGE BOSS
(career advice to the buckskinned
Dillards)

"Mitch, you need to get yourself
some nice shoes."
—BEA JAYNE
(career advice to her son)

"Every time you ever accommodate some son of a bitch,
you end up holding the shitty end of the stick"
—A CLARENCE WEBB Saying
(Dean's dad)

"Now he thinks he can ride a bicycle!"
TOWN LOONEY No. II, denigrating 'Bicycle Jim,'
TOWN LOONEY No. I – Salem, Mo.

"I can't even fix a friggin' toaster."
—GREG MORRIS of *MISSION IMPOSSIBLE*
(being interviewed by Mitch for Dick Clark)

"Mitch, have you boys got them hogs washed yet?"
—DENVER PYLE
(practising the character for "BRISCOE DARLING")

"I don't like people lookin' at me when I'm not
working."
—ANDY GRIFFITH
(when Dean asked why he didn't drive a Rolls Royce)

"Aw, they don't really do that. . . do they?"
—LITTLE ROY LEWIS
(upon looking at pictures taken in a
Tijuana sex show, shown him by
Sonny Osborne before Roy's
wedding)

"Only thing I done longer than this is breathe"
—MOMS MABLEY
(talking about show business)

"Are you somebody?"
—FAN
(questioning a DILLARD on tour with the BYRDS)

MITCH: How many cats do you have Frances?
FRANCES BAVIER: Fifteen
MITCH: Why Fifteen?
FRANCES: Why not?
—MAYBERRY'S AUNT BEE

"I dreamed the perfect song idea and wrote it down
on a pad next to the bed. When I woke up I looked
and it said; 'Boy meets girl.' "
—JOHN HARTFORD

"Me and Oswald have been married fifty years"
—ROY ACUFF

"Then I shan't pick a note in your country."
—NORMAN BLAKE
(Guitarist from Georgia, after very British-speaking
guards at the Canadian border said he couldn't enter
until they inspected his guitar case for contraband.)

"A little success makes a physical change in your mind and body."
—ROGER MILLER
(explaining his $400 shoes and new Armani suit to Mitch)

"He knows better than to aggravate me too far. I'll just by God go back to the coal mine."
—JOE STEWART
(on working for Bill Monroe)

"It wouldn't hurt to tune that thing just a little."
—KENNY BAKER – FIDDLER
(being mountain-polite to a picker at a festival jam)

"Are you somebody?"
—FAN,
(questioning a DILLARD on ELTON JOHN Tour)

"Bill Monroe said there isn't anything over there fit to eat."
—DOUG DILLARD
(stocking up on canned chili for our first trip to Japan)

"Press LOBBY, that's the flush button for these places."
—PAT PAULSEN – COMEDIAN
(on a WILLIAM MORRIS AGENCY elevator.)

"Just what you need in this town; a big horn!"
—"MAMA" CASS ELLIOT
(Taking THE DILLARDS around Greewich Village, NY)

"Boys, this is Ernie's [Tennessee Ernie Ford's] show. I'm going to wear a tux, and I think you boys should too."
—ANDY GRIFFITH

"I think the tuxedos are becoming to you guys, and don't worry about the straw bales and wagon wheels, that's just Hollywood."
—WILLIAM MORRIS AGENT
THE JUDY GARLAND SHOW

"When you say good-bye to somebody important, say, Wy-uri koto shen-iodai kudes-sai!"
—TIM COONEY, World Traveler
(Advising Mitch about Japanese customs)
(translation: "Don't do anything I wouldn't do")

"A singer is only as good as his whiskey"
—TEX WILLAMS

"You guys are going to be the next big act."
—DICKIE SMOTHERS

"Wait a minute— I've got a cramp in my head!"
—DOUG DILLARD

"Boys, you sure are a long way from the house!"
—CALIFORNIA GAS STATION ATTENDANT
(Noticing the Dillards Missouri plates)

"You guys kill me! You always act like this job is the only one you'll ever get."
—HOLLYWOOD AGENT
(advising the Dillards)

" Let's stop for some nice lard loaf"
—DEAN WEBB
(commenting on a Texas diner)

"A farting horse will never tire, and a farting man's the man to hire!"
—A CLARENCE WEBB Saying
(Dean's dad)

"Come on! Everybody Sing!"
—PETE SEEGER
 (Urging Ralph and Carter Stanley, dignified Mountain people to sing along on "All the Fish in the Ocean.")

"I'd just like to pick him up by the hair and shake him till he wets."
—NORMAN BLAKE
(talking about a slippery festival promoter)

"It took me ten yeahs to get from the guttah up on the coib."
—NEW ORLEANS DILLARD FAN
(explaining his upbringing)

"They ain't a rat hole in the world so big he wouldn't try to pound sand down it."
—OZARK FATHER
(talking about his profligate son)

"That's fine, you can go set down over there now."
—BILL MONROE
(Cueing Dee Dee Prestige—Female Vocalist singing with his band at Opryland)

(sings) " 'They took me to the hos-pit-al
And all my friends gathered round me
They said I was the world's only living dead man. . .'
    "That's the ballad of the wrecked carpenter, that one is. . . they say I've wrote several more that are going to be hits."
—OB SHUNK, Missourian
(on his mail order investment in a Nashville song writing career)

"Why hell, they've bladed this since I was down it."
—RED BARTON – Salem, Mo.
(commenting on attempting a totally washed out wagon road)

"It's whoever you want it to be, Mitch."
—ALLAN MUNDE
(At a Bluegrass awards ceremony after I had opened
the envelope with my buck knife.)

"This is going to open new doors for you guys"
—WILLIAM MORRIS AGENT
(booking the Dillards into a Vegas lounge)

"Godalmighty, if that girl was to fall down, she'd be
halfway home"
—JOE STEWART
(remarking on a tall girl at a festival)

"Why I wouldn't be afraid to drive this thing to
California"
—FREDDY WHITACRE - Salem, Mo.
(Used Car Salesman)

"If you'd eat grass, I'd just leave you!"
—GRANDPA JONES
(Speaking to a jeep he had accidentally built a fence
around)

"What kind of intelligence do you expect from a cow?
It spends its whole life studying the two square feet of
grass in front of it."
—RANDY CARNETT – Salem, Mo.
(cattle raiser)

" A Holstein cow will wander around twenty years, just looking for a place to die"
—DAIRY FARMER – Salem, Mo.

"These Indiana people don't get excited about nothing. They wouldn't go around the corner to see a piss-ant eat a bale of hay!"
—JOE STEWART
(Bill Monroe's band)

"Old Simmer looks like he's been a-sortin' bobcats."
—DEWEY BYRD – Former Salem police chief
(commenting on a tavern fight)

 "Why on earth would you take a sack lunch to a banquet?"
—GOLDEN STATE BOYS BASS PLAYER
(on being asked if he was going to take his wife on tour)

"Now you put in one bay leaf, jist the one, mind, or ye'll rurn the whole damn bilin' of it!"
—JUNIOR SAMPLES
(Cooking twenty pounds of shrimp for a snack)

"I think I've died and gone to Branson."
—PAT PAULSEN - COMEDIAN

"I've got a mind like a steel sieve"
—DIANA JAYNE
(on her retentive memory for names)

"I guess you think I'm just another magician-banjo player who makes balloon animals"
—STEVE MARTIN
(speaking to an early club audience)

"He's a good enough deer hunter, but comes to shooting one he couldn't hit a barn if he was inside it."
—WILBERN PACE – Salem, Mo.

"He'll work if you tell him what to do. But if you don't tell him, he'll just set around like a turd in a dead eddy."
—RED BARTON – Salem, Mo.

I can't decide whether to be a fry cook or a double-naught spy."
—PHILLIP ZISKE
(Salem teenager circa 1975)

"ORPY? What the hell is an ORPY?"
—SONNY OSBORNE
(upon discovering that the sign painter had misspelled Grand 'Ol Opry on their new tour bus.)

"And then we pray?"
—JAPANESE BLUEGRASS PICKER
(after I had explained how the MC would introduce his group.)

" Ross All My Money But A Two Dorrow Beer And
I'm On My Wrong Journey Home"
—JAPANESE SINGER
(dedicating a song to the "Dirruhds" [Dillards] at a
Japanese Folk Club)

ANDY GRIFFITH: (Rehearsing greeting to Maggie
Peterson's character Charlene Wash on 'Divorce
Mountain Style')
"Well, Charlene Darling Wash!"
DENVER PYLE: (aside to the Darling boys)
"I wonder if that's a greeting or a stage direction?"

"Are you somebody?"
—FAN
 (questioning a Dillard while on a rock tour with,
among others, Three Dog Night, and Mitch Ryder
and the Detroit Wheels)

"Keeping an eye on Junior is kind of like having an
alligator in your john boat—it's hard not to."
—JUNIOR SAMPLES' MANAGER
(on Junior staying at my house for a week)

"I've cut a world of brush but this is the first time I've
ever plainted any."
—GOOB NORRIS – Ozark neighbor
(while helping me plant pine trees on my property)

"Kids like that ought to be kept in a barrel and fed through the bung till they're twelve. Then you drive in the bung.
—ANONYMOUS
(on teenagers)

I'm going to conclude these quotes with a Dorman Steelman story, because I want to point out a moral of sorts to this glimpse into the way we all say funny things. Dorman, being the judge I mentioned earlier, who advised a lawyer on shaky ground that his "dog wouldn't hunt." Dorman earned lot of admiration and public respect during his years as circuit judge because, as his old friend Walter Prugh explained one time, "Dorman knows all the big words but he hasn't forgot how good the little ones sound."

Dorman loves his colorful native language, and he told me about being a young lawyer and representing a Shannon County man, Danny Staples, in a tilt with the U.S. Government over some of the Staples family land they wanted at about a third of its value. (Ozarkians love this story because Danny Staples later on became [and still is] a member of the Missouri Senate.)

Since Dorman had battled Uncle Sam before with success, Danny asked him to represent him at a meeting the government agency had set up in Cape Girardeau, Missouri.

"We stayed at the Sunnyside Motel," Dorman said," but all the Government lawyers and witnesses were being put up at the Ramada Inn, over in the high rent district. You could sort of figure it was going to be like that; big against little."

That night the two men left to meet this impressive array of Washington lawyers and "experts" in their Ramada suite for what was to be an informal "pre-hearing." On the way to the hotel Dorman told Danny, "Now Danny I know you're high tempered and outspoken, but please don't say anything. Let them concentrate on me and what I have to say on your behalf."

When they got there, the government people sat in the only chairs and had covered the bed with papers so that the visitors would have to stand, which Dorman was used to doing. Danny finally sat patiently on the floor in a corner while Dorman laid out his case before the Government legal forces. "We went on and on," Dorman said, "and I kept an eye on Danny, stuck there in the corner. By 4:30 in the morning I knew he was sick of listening to lawyers. I got everything said that I needed to and presented them with Danny's offer. I turned to him and said, "What do you think Danny? And Danny got to his feet and said the funniest thing anyone ever said to a bunch like that. He said "Dorman, it's their possum, now let them wool it."

Dorman and Danny won that case so long ago, and it is a good example of the way Ozarkians have managed to hold their own in a world that minces cultures like making sausage. I'd like to see all of us do that; hold what we've got in the way of colorful, interesting speech so that we don't end up a nation of TV anchor people.

Noticing the different ways that people talk and appreciating them isn't the work of anthropologists, it's the pleasure of Americans in general and you owe it to yourself to listen. I would, but I'm getting deafer than a snake.

So it's your possum,
now you wool it!

257

W. Y. Ozark Words

Warrant *Stand good for* —
"*I'll warrant he can walk ye lather-jawed.*"

We'uns *We (all of us)* —
"*We'uns all went to the doins.*"

Whilst *While* —
"*I do my bakin' the fore part of the day whilst the old man's still abed.*"

Withouten *Unless* —
"*He'll be there, withouten he dies on the way or somethin'.*"

Wonders me *Makes me wonder* —
"*It wonders me why God invented these cancers.*"

Wonderment *(as a noun-adjective)* —
"*How he got elected is a wonderment to me.*"

Ye *You - you all* —
"*I'm tellin' ye the word with the bark on it!*"

Yit *Even now* —
"*I was a democrat then and I'm a democrat yit!*"

Yon - Yonder *Over there* —
"*Yon tree's the biggest Chinkapin in the whole of Missouri.*"
"*The whole of yonder mountain is one big cedar brake.*"

You'uns *You (all of you)* —
"*You'uns come, stay all night!*"

Chapter Twelve

How Everything Is Going So Far

In naming this chapter I was reminded of an old friend who was getting married for the third time and I was his best man, hanging on to the ring and being supportive. His first two marriages had been disasters but like me he always hoped for the best. In the middle of the ceremony he leaned over to me for an aside I've always remembered; "How do you think this is going so far?"

I figure to stick in a couple of my own thoughts in this, my fifth big plunge into a book length project. Writing a book is a lot like putting the whole farm in corn instead of a half dozen crops to even the odds on Missouri weather. I'm hoping that a lot of strangers will like my kind of Ozark humor enough to get me through another winter.

The reason I call it *Home Grown Stories and Home Fried Lies* is probably—as much as anything—to establish the difference between them in my own mind. I didn't want to do "whoppers" or "windies" because everybody has heard these legendary things and people from every state have their own. Like the Paul Bunyan stories from up north, these are classic examples of folklore. Davy Crockett or maybe Daniel Boone who kills five different animals with one shot and wading to get his kills, ends up with his boots full of fish. Now that's folklore, where you're allowed to lie because everybody did it for years and got away with it.

Ozarkians are more subtle when stretching the truth. Of course we lie with impunity, but it's more of a straight faced formal kind of lie, conversationally told lies like; "Old man Sellars farm's so steep he has to look up the chimney to see if his cows are coming home to milk."

This might seem to be a wild exaggeration at first glance, but it is qualified by reality. An Ozarkian would never tell a stranger something so outlandish as, "Old man Sellars' farm's so steep his shadow fell out of his cornfield and broke its leg," because that would be a transparent lie. These we leave to people from Texas and other windy places.

*O*ne of the reasons I like to use Zeke Dooley as a storyteller is that Zeke knows how to tell lies effectively, as in this interview for *Today's Farmer*, years ago. . . .

> **Mitch:** Zeke, what do you know about hail storms?
>
> **Zeke:** Enough that I don't crave to be out in one without a hat.
>
> **Mitch:** What was the worst one you've seen?
>
> **Zeke:** Spring of nineteen-and-ought-five. It come a hail storm that blowed sideways. Hailstones wasn't even round—they was long and sharp as needles. They'd go through a choppin' block.
>
> **Mitch:** I've never heard of that.
>
> **Zeke:** Hit's gospel. And wind with it, so strong I thought it was fixin' to blow the barn over. Would have too, except

that hail punched so many holes in the side it looked like a Booger County road sign. Let the wind right through, you see.

Mitch: Long and sharp hailstones. Isn't that unusual?

Zeke: Sonny, I've saw ever shape they is. I've saw round ones, square ones and some no more shape than a oyster and bigger'n a churn.

Mitch: I bet those did some damage.

Zeke: You hain't no idee. That's why folks all had root cellars back in them times, called 'em fraidy holes. Hailstorms these days don't amount to nothing.

Mitch: Didn't people get killed?

Zeke: All the time. Onliest reason I'm still around, I always div' for the fraidy hole first. I lost several cousins to hailstorms when we was kids. Slow on their feet, you know, and had nothin' but livestock to git under.

Mitch: How about the grown-ups?

Zeke: They had sense enough to git under something or wear a head kivver. But you cain't tell a kid nothing. I can still hear my sister Tewkie yell at her grandkids. "Now if you'uns kids is a-goin' to play in that hailstorm, you put a hubcap on this minit."

Mitch: Tell me about the square hailstones. Were they really square, Zeke?

Zeke: Why yes, and big as bricks, too. One year the corn was a foot high and it come a hailstorm. Them big old hail bricks driv' the whole crop into the ground like nails.

Mitch: Lost the whole crop, did you?

Zeke: Well actual, no. That field was pounded smoother than a schoolmarm's whoosis fer a week, but then it come a shower of rain and here come that corn back up out of them holes. It had been driv' into the ground so fast it didn't hurt it none.

Mitch: Zeke, it's hard to imagine that.

Zeke: You ain't tryin' hard enough. They have pitchers of a straw that'us driv' through a fence post. Now I'll own up to stretchin' the truth a tad. But that's kind of like drinkin'. A man who don't stretch the truth or drink don't belong to be tellin' about Missouri weather in the first place. And nobody'd listen if he did.

*I*t always seemed to me that Zeke was useful in telling a home fried lie like that one. Of course this was just warming up for his really outrageous stretchers, like this one about Native Americans that I used for a spoof on Branson, Missouri. This atrocity was actually recorded on tape for *Stories From Home,* another project I did for Dan Randant at Wildstone Media.

Mitch: Zeke, do you know anything about the Indians who used to live around here?

Zeke: Know about 'em? Why shore I know about 'em. My connection on my grandmaw's side was partial Cherokee. Used to be serval Cherokees in these parts.

Mitch: Well maybe you'd know then. Were the Cherokee hunting or farming Indians?

Zeke: Well fur's I know they done anything they could to git by like everbody else in the Ozarks. This ain't much country fer specialists.

Mitch: So they both hunted and fished.

Zeke: Yeah, and sold stuff to the tourists. Snake oil and nostrums and sich, peddled a little real estate.

Mitch: Zeke, I'm talking about the Indians two hundred years ago, not modern tribes.

Zeke: Well that's what I'm a talkin' about too. Them old time Indians wasn't nobody's fools. My grandmaw said that her old daddy sold chalk dogs and cement bird baths to the early settlers down here, plus he had a food concession down on White River. His name was Chief Taneycomo. You've heerd of the lake they named after him ain't chee?

Mitch: Zeke, Taneycomo isn't an Indian name.

Zeke: What makes ye think it ain't?

Mitch: Because it's an abbreviation for Taney County, Missouri.

Zeke: Well, if you want to think that. All I know is what my grandmaw told me.

Mitch: Dammit Zeke, the Corps of Engineers named that lake!

Zeke: Who you goin' to believe, them or my grandmaw?

Mitch: Well anyway, tell me more about the Cherokee Indians. I always thought it was the Osage that lived in this part of the country.

Zeke: Oh well, they was a scatterin' of them too, but they wasn't no hands to dog trade and horse swap like Cherokees was. Cherokees had a place up by Alley Spring where the pioneers could git their wagons painted. Any wagon, any color fer 39 shotgun hulls and a skinnin' knife.

Mitch: Zeke they didn't have shotgun shells back then.

Zeke: Whatever. Maybe it was 39 coon hides. Anyway them Indians was sharp dealers and when they seen the white men was fixin' to build a road, they'd set in to sell him the right of way and string out a mess of tradin' posts along it to sell travelers all manner of plunder, like coon skin caps and lunch meat and little bow'n arrs fer the children and hand made moccasins and molasses candy and I don't know whut-tall plunder.

Mitch: Zeke, you're making all this up.

Zeke: On my word as a partial Indian! They'd put on big war dainces fer the tourists too, whatever they wanted to see. My grandmaw said she run the hot dog concession at one of them pow wows.

Mitch: Hot dogs, Zeke? You claim she sold hot dogs?

Zeke: You gonna tell me they didn't have dogs back then?

Mitch: Never mind.

Zeke: Well what I'm a-sayin' is that your Indians was supposed to be ignorant savages.

Mitch: Not so, huh?

Zeke: What they was, was native Ozarkers a-makin' do with what they had. My great-great uncle on Grandmaw's side, old Whatch-a-gimme, he run a canoe rental up by Pulltite Spring. Rented as many as ten canoes a day.

Mitch That many, huh? I bet it was crowded.

Zeke: Wall to wall birch bark. He crowded hisself out of business. Folks got to claimin' they couldn't git no sense of unspoiled nature with all them canoes bangin' together. They quit comin' down and he went broke.

Mitch: What did he do then?

Zeke: What most of us do. Sold out to the gover-mint and waited for better times.

Mitch: I bet he had to wait a while for that.

Zeke: Yeah but what's time to an Indian?

Mitch: Thanks for the history lesson Zeke

Zeke: Well they say history repeats itself. I know I do.

I liked using Zeke's take it or leave it attitude about the windy lies he told, as opposed to the home grown story like the one that follows. Both kinds of stories had a place in the Ozark culture, one composed of whimsy, the other of fact. I wrote this one down as soon as I heard it, but had to wait ten years to sell it to anybody.

Back home in the Ozarks my friend Lester Adamick set in to raise every kind of animal he could, as sort of a curiosity thing. He mostly just wanted to see if he could raise something profitable that would be more fun to fool with than cows. He tried all the wild Missouri animals like bobcats and deer, and even had a mountain lion, and fighting chickens, and wild turkeys, and a bear or two, plus some coyotes. He owned lots of land and made big pens for all these animals. People would come to gawk at them and wonder why anyone would want to keep these things, and it was all-around fun for Lester who dances to a different drummer than most.

One time he decided to go into the ostrich business and ordered a mated pair; cost him $5000, and that was a lot of money then—and now. He could hardly wait for them to be delivered and he made an acre-big pen out of chain link fence, eight feet high.

We were friends of the Adamicks and my wife had read up a little on ostriches. She warned him about them. She said, "Lester, those things have big old feet as hard as anvils, and they can kick the guts out of a lion and I've read that they will. If one of them chases you with a view to kicking you, lie down flat and you won't be a threat to it any more. Their brains are about the size of a new potato and they will forget all about you as soon as you lie down."

When the delivery truck got the ostriches unloaded, Lester gave the birds a little time to settle down and then went out there with a bucket of corn to feed them, like he was used to feeding chickens or turkeys.

Now most Ozark people take the Bible literally and Lester had read in Genesis that man was to have dominion over all creatures that walked, flew, or crawled. He had never doubted that he could dominate anything in the animal line and went out to feed these ostriches with total confidence. He hadn't any more than stepped into the pen, however, than the old buck ostrich spotted him and lit out for him. Lester sensed that he wasn't just trotting over to get acquainted either, but came in a head down gallop that said 'Attack Mode.' Lester said, "He didn't look right out of his eyes," which is a good Ozark term meaning he looked crazy.

Lester remembered what my wife had told him and flopped down flatter than grease on a skillet. Sure enough the ostrich calmed down, peered around a little for the tall threat and then wandered off back to his mate.

For an Ozarkian who believes that man has dominion over all creatures, this was a blow to Lester's pride and prostrating himself in front of an animal had never been Lester's habit. So after a while he got up with his bucket and strode off toward that ostrich to establish his biblical superiority.

This time the ostrich whistled out a kick at him, which if it had connected, would have torn his head off. Lester dodged in time and laid down flat, and pretty soon the ostrich wandered off again.

By this time, Lester's stinger was about half out, and when the ostrich wasn't looking he ran over and got one of those ten foot steel posts he had left over from building the fence. He put his corn down and swung the post around like a ball bat and yelled, "All right big boy, come and get it!" The ostrich did, and when he got in range Lester took a big swing and laid that steel post right up alongside his head, and down went the ostrich, shedding feathers like "sawing through a pillow," Lester said. He kicked and flopped a little and then got real still.

About that time Lester got to thinking about the incredible money he had just paid for what was now 300 pounds of meat. He started walking toward the gate and was looking back feeling pretty dejected, when that ostrich kind of shook himself and raised up his head all wobbly and snakey, and staggered up to his feet. He moped around for a minute and then staggered off toward his mate, "about a bubble off level," Lester said, and he saw the fool thing was all right.

He went back in the house and asked his wife, "Fleeta Mae, where did you put the cherry brandy?" and she said, "Why Lester, you don't drink at nine o'clock in the morning!"

And he said, "Well it's a special occasion, celebrating something we won't have to do."

"Like what?" asked Fleeta.

"You and me came *that close*," said Lester, "having to learn how to make ostrich-hide purses for a living."

Stories like 'Lester And The Ostrich' were Ozark stories from home, fun to tell friends, but almost impossible to sell to a market. I wrote them down anyway, and saved them. I even got what I think of as an additional bank-shot off this story when I told it to a friend whose wife was one of the most pessimistic, doom-ridden people I had ever met, and her total reaction to Lester's ostrich adventure was; "Well, I guess that's the way he'll go." That topped the story itself for hilarity as far as I was concerned and I made the lady an immediate candidate for the character of Zeke Dooley's wife.

Long suffering and always expecting the worst, Perletta Dooley has been a perfect foil for Zeke, who pretty much does as he pleases. She is the type of Ozark woman who reads the obituaries before any other part of the paper, predicts worst scenarios in any situation and says things like, "I allus can remember Zeke'l's birthday because it was the same month and day as the big freshet that warshed away my Granpa Cargill and a Poland Chiny hog, may he rest in peace." or, "That boy never did look right to me," when a neighbor kid is arrested for something. I figured that anyone who had read Charles Dickens would recognize the character as a Mrs. Gummidge type, "a lone, lorn creature not long for this world," who would probably outlive everybody in the entire book.

Here is Perletta at her best, taken from a story I wrote for *The Missouri Conservationist*, 'Zeke Dooley and The Inedible Deer'. . . .

> **Mitch:** Hi folks, you picked a good day to sit on the porch.
> **Perletta:** Well, while it lasts. This kind of day breeds weather I allus heerd. "Warm days in September means hard times in November," I've heerd said.
> **Zeke:** If it stays as dry as Perletta, hit'll do.

> **Mitch:** I brought some tradin' goods down. Figured I'd swap for one of Perletta's venison recipes and maybe one of your funny stories.
>
> **Perletta:** Why I'm no great hand to cook a deer, but mamma had a receipt or two you could copy off. All the best cooks is named on tombstones and venison don't taste like it used to no ways anymore.

Perletta is simply wonderful as the type of Ozark farm wife who expects the worst all the time and anticipates death with a collector's enthusiasm. "I keep my receipts in the Bible," she tells her listener, "next to the obituaries of them that has gone on to a better world."

In reading back over the stories I have so loosely divided into two categories, I realize that over a fifty year period of writing down funny stuff, I have a lot of short humor that falls through the cracks. Maybe I should have called these Home Made Commentaries but that sounds too cute. An example. . . .

Douglas Dillard never could understand why Dean Webb was so particular about selecting hotel rooms for us on the road. Dean was always careful to check for disappointing things like cheap toilet paper, low wattage bulbs, coarse towels, and a general lack of comfort consideration on the part of the host. There were times when we would sit in the bus for ten minutes while Dean checked things out. On one of these occasions Douglas, who was starved, said, "I don't know what takes Dean so long, it don't take me long to look at a horse-shoe."

It cracked us all up but I don't suppose one out of a dozen people hearing it would have known why. He was quoting a 100 year-old story about a loafer hanging around a blacksmith shop who idly picks up a horseshoe the smith has flung on the ground to cool. Of course it burns him and one of the other loafers says, "Hot, was it?" And the first loafer says, "No, it wasn't that, it just don't take me long to look at a horseshoe."

I didn't want to tackle these kinds of stories because the explanation would belabor the thing, and yet this is sort of the gist of Ozark humor. I decided to just tell things that I thought would be funny to anybody. Like my wife's uncle Ray, who told the census taker; "You see those two mountains sticking up yonder? When I came here those were holes in the ground." Or another relative who, seeing the vast chasm of the Grand Canyon for the first time said, "They better fence this place off before somebody gets hurt."

This sly use of exaggeration isn't just native to the Ozarks, but it is so typical of us that I wanted to tell a lot of these stories about so-called experts who could take pleasure in making fun of themselves.

Like the story about Steve Bryson and the time he tried to teach his mule obedience.

Steve was one of those patient people who are good with hounds or mules because he took the time to figure out what would make sense to an animal. Steve never expected mules or hounds to think like a human and tried to deal with them on their own terms; reward and punishment.

Steve taught me a lot about mules and always emphasized that a good mule trainer never lost his temper, no matter what stubbornness the mule displayed.

"A mule," he told me, "is like a three year old kid, it wants to find out how far it can get away with things. Once it puts two and two together, a mule can reason."

One evening before a coon hunt, Steve decided to saddle up his jumping mule, Benny. Tying his long reins to the door handle of the truck, he tossed a blanket over the mule's back. Benny was one of those contrary creatures I always tried to avoid but Steve took him on as a challenge to his training skills. He liked a mule with spirit and Benny had plenty of that. This time Benny decided he didn't like his saddle blanket, and each time Steve tossed the blanket over the mule's back, Benny would flip it off, or snatch it off with his teeth before Steve could get the saddle mounted.

After this had happened three times, Steve, breaking his own number one rule, lost his temper. He put down the saddle, picked up a stick from the woodpile and whacked Benny right between the ears with it. Stunned, the mule let him put the saddle blanket on and stood shivering while Steve apologized, petted him and calmed him down.

"Now Benny," he said, "I'm sorry I lost my temper and whacked you, but sometimes you'd make Jesus slap his mama."

Letting the mule think about it, Steve went back in the shop to get his saddlebags and his miner's light for coon hunting. On the way out he picked up an ax handle he had bought for a friend and was carrying everything to the truck when Benny spotted the ax handle, put two and two together and got in the truck. Not the bed, but the cab, through the open window.

Steve described it to me. "He was half in the passenger side and half out, with his head stuck in the steering wheel, and it took me a half hour to ease him back out a little at a time. You wouldn't have believed me talking to that mule, promising him all manner of outlandish stuff and trying to get his hooves off the gear shift and out of the seat cushions, and all the time easing him back out the window."

I could tell that Steve had learned a great lesson from this exercise in mule psychology because he told me; "A man with mules should never own a Cadillac."

Having said all this I suppose it's time to let you go on to the final part of my meandering; hopefully leaving you with a few more funny things to laugh at.

Looking back over these chapters I realize that I have very likely confused any reader trying to keep track of the time element in my book. I finally decided that it wouldn't make a lot of difference to people who would pick this up liking Diana's cover design or maybe just grabbing something to read on an airplane, like I would. People on airplanes need all the entertainment they can get and aren't too particular what they read as long at it keeps their minds off the fallible quality of machinery.

I have wondered how much personal life to put in the book, and decided to put in just enough to let you know that I certainly didn't do all this by myself. I have been married three times and each one of these marriages was important and worthwhile. I don't want to complicate the funny stuff by including my own genealogy, but it seems to me that I have just sort of skated through 70 years here without any landmarks and should establish some credibility.

My first wife introduced me to the Ozarks, as I have told you, and is the mother of our two children. After 21 years, with the kids grown, we went our separate ways and each remarried. I married another Missouri girl who, after the log house burned—and our life together with it, went on to earn her Ph.D. and find her own career. She was a wise and delightful companion, who said things like; "The five elements are earth, air, fire, water and gristle." We also were married for 21 years.

These are valuable people and I know we learned a lot from our time together. Like my student in Cross School advised, we simply decided not to "spend 50 years sittin' on the blister."

Marriage, in my experience at least, has always been sort of an enigma that I can't help but think is a lot like family relationships; when people decide that blood is thicker than water, they get techious with that concept, like brothers who don't agree.

As a matter of fact, when brothers do fall out they can usually fight nastier than anyone. It is never a good idea for anyone to intervene in these quarrels, because both of them will then turn their wrath on the peace-maker. My sister-in-law used to tell about her two cousins who were always disagreeing over something and one morning got into it at the breakfast table. They actually came to blows and when one of them picked up a butcher knife from the chopping block, the other one grabbed a stick of stove wood to defend himself. Their old daddy decided to intervene and leaping between the two said "Now boys. . . ." soothingly, at which point one hit him with the stick of wood and the other one stabbed him.

Which reminds me of another story told by my friend Charlie, a native of Holiday, Missouri, where people were known to disagree about The War Between The States. He told me of a couple of great-great cousins, brothers, who were given leave from the war to come home for Thanksgiving. They were officers, one Union and the other Confederate, and in honor of the occasion were cordial and in a great good humor until somebody brought up the war, at which point they began arguing, drew their pistols and shot each other to death at the dinner table.

It has always seemed to me that marriage too, has its limits and I'm sure it would be a good idea to stop short of shooting each other at the Thanksgiving table.

My present wife, also my friend and partner, Diana, is an artist, and my long sought-after team mate. I'm sure that I will take forevermore to look at this particular horse shoe. After four years of courtship by mail we finally got together and were married at the Story's Creek one room schoolhouse at Alley Spring, a place captured in time and spirit by the Forest Service for just such an occasion.

Our careers have meshed just right, we laugh at each other's speech (Diana's from Texas), and we admire each other's work so much we have a built-in support system.

As I mentioned early on, I am certainly a poor authority on marriages but I think what has made this one successful is the blending of enthusiasms. Diana loves the Ozarks and Bluegrass music, and I seem to have spent most of my life involved with both, while refusing to take either one very seriously. When you love something a lot, you better be prepared to see all sides of it. "Even a peacock's got an asshole," as my favorite in-law aunt used to say.

Of my favorite things, Bluegrass music, has always aggravated me as much as it pleased me because the people who love it the most have never ceased arguing about it and picking at it. There is an old joke about that. . . .

How many Bluegrass fans does it take to change a light bulb? The answer: Four of them; one to change the bulb and three to talk about how much better the old bulb was.

The longer I live, the more I realize that when we become specialists of any kind, we tend to get ponderous about our specialty, believing that we have some unique dispensation to preach about it.

In trying to complete this book as best I can, I keep thinking back to old "Goob" Norris who delighted in looking down over the patchwork quilt pattern of his crops in the fields, 20 acres of alfalfa, ten of oats, six of rye, forty of corn and maybe an acre of sorghum just for the fun of it. He never became bored with farming because each crop was a guessing game and he said, "I just like to watch things grow."

We could all do worse than watching things grow, be it children, a way of life, a state of mind, a book, or a bunch of illustrations. I hope that they are all meant to somehow leave a statement about why we were put here, and what sort of crop we made of our time.

The truth is that Diana is my other, wiser half, a factor that occurs in lots of lucky marriages. To expect that a sense of humor will guide every marriage is to ask too much of our creator, but according to mountain lore,

"Even a blind hog finds an acorn sometimes."

Word List Comments

My Ozark Word list isn't complete and never will be. I have found myself adding to it every time I go home. If I was ever going to finish this book I had to either live another seventy years, or go with a partial list and leave out every day things like—*I'll not*, rather than *I won't*; and *take a lick about*, instead of *take turns*. I left out a lot of old usages like:

"*That dog Fannie, is well named; she arrives last, but she'll show up* **erelong**."

"*I'll not* **gainsay** *what you're telling me.*"

"*I'll meet you* **a-Thursday**."

If you see that I've left something out, add stuff of your own. I'm nary bit *jealous hearted* and besides, I may be coming down with *old-timer's disease* and just forgot.

Mitch Jayne lives in Columbia, Missouri, with his wife, Diana. This is his fifth book.

Mitch writes a weekly humor column for *The Current Wave* newspaper in Eminence, Missouri, and has a humor column for *Today's Farmer Magazine*, and also writes articles for *The Missouri Conservationist* magazine.

When not touring with The Dillards or writing, Mitch gives talks throughout the state of Missouri on Ozark speech.

Diana is a freelance artist and illustrator.

AUDIOCASSETTES AVAILABLE BY MITCH JAYNE:

STORIES FROM HOME
VOL. I & II

Over 2 hours of the wit and wisdom of Mitch Jayne
on 2 audiocassettes. Listen and laugh as Mitch
narrates some of his favorite "stories from home"
like, *Yard Sales, The Floater's Guide,
Ozark Language*, and many more.

$15 plus $3 s&h

OLD FISH HAWK

Mitch's touching tale of one of the last Osage Indians
and his quest to return to the land of his ancestors.
Over 4-1/2 hours on 4 cassettes
with sound effects and original music.

$20 plus $4 s&h

Send Check or money order to:

WILDSTONE MEDIA
PO BOX 511580
ST. LOUIS, MO 63151

CALL 1-800-296-1918
to order with MC/Visa

www.wildstonemedia.com